A Candlelight Ecstasy Romance®

"ONCE I GOT SO DISTRACTED WATCHING YOU, I ALMOST SWALLOWED A PAPER CLIP," BANNING ADMITTED.

"Fortunately I can perform the Heimlich maneuver if that should ever happen," Riley said demurely.

"If I'd known you were so talented, I'd have faked something."

"Really?" She ran the tip of her tongue over her lip.

Banning took an unsteady breath. "I know what you're up to, you little tease. You're driving me crazy!" He bent his head and placed tiny kisses along her neck.

"Why, Banning," she said breathlessly, "whatever are you doing?"

"If you don't know, I must be doing it wrong."

"Oh, no," she murmured as his sure hands pulled her close. "You're doing everything just *perfectly. . . .*"

CANDLELIGHT ECSTASY CLASSIC ROMANCES

CANDLELIGHT ECSTASY ROMANCES®

QUANTITY SALES

Most Dell Books are available at special quantity discounts when purchased in bulk by corporations, organizations, and special-interest groups. Custom imprinting or excerpting can also be done to fit special needs. For details write: Dell Publishing Co., Inc., 1 Dag Hammarskjold Plaza, New York, NY 10017, Attn.: Special Sales Dept., or phone: (212) 605-3319.

INDIVIDUAL SALES

Are there any Dell Books you want but cannot find in your local stores? If so, you can order them directly from us. You can get any Dell book in print. Simply include the book's title, author, and ISBN number, if you have it, along with a check or money order (no cash can be accepted) for the full retail price plus 75¢ per copy to cover shipping and handling. Mail to: Dell Readers Service, Dept. FM, 6 Regent Street, Livingston, N.J. 07039.

FANCY FOOTWORK

Cory Kenyon

A CANDLELIGHT ECSTASY ROMANCE®

Published by
Dell Publishing Co., Inc.
1 Dag Hammarskjold Plaza
New York, New York 10017

Dell ® TM 681510, Dell Publishing Co., Inc.

Candlelight Ecstasy Romance®, 1,203,540, is a registered
trademark of Dell Publishing Co., Inc., New York, New York.

ISBN: 0-440-12445-X

Printed in the United States of America

May 1987

10 9 8 7 6 5 4 3 2 1

WFH

To Regan Forest, the "I Love Lucy" of Tucson, who knows about nails and wallpaper. Her creative approach to life keeps us laughing.

To Dave Nadworny, the hero to everyone who can't keep their bankbook straight.

To Our Readers:

We have been delighted with your enthusiastic response to Candlelight Ecstasy Romances®, and we thank you for the interest you have shown in this exciting series.

In the upcoming months we will continue to present the distinctive sensuous love stories you have come to expect only from Ecstasy. We look forward to bringing you many more books from your favorite authors and also the very finest work from new authors of contemporary romantic fiction.

As always, we are striving to present the unique, absorbing love stories that you enjoy most—books that are more than ordinary romance. Your suggestions and comments are always welcome. Please write to us at the address below.

Sincerely,

The Editors
Candlelight Romances
1 Dag Hammarskjold Plaza
New York, New York 10017

FANCY
FOOTWORK

CHAPTER ONE

His solitude ended tomorrow. Banning rolled away from his oak desk and leaned back in the swivel chair. He didn't put his feet up, although the temptation was still there, years after renouncing such adolescent behavior.

But the desk was expensive, paid for with hard-won accounts, and his leather shoes were recently polished. Black shoe polish didn't do much for light oak.

Did Riley Dugan put his feet on the desk after a long day? What sort of office habits would an Irish traveling shoe salesman have? Banning was curious. Dugan's letters from D.C. had been business-like, but there was an undercurrent of—what? Zest? Humor? Maybe it was the name of Dugan's business that aroused Banning's curiosity. The name was a little strange.

Banning hoped his new office partner wasn't a clown, but maybe that didn't matter, either. Banning figured the guy would be out selling shoes most of the time. Just so he paid his rent the first of every month. And didn't smoke cigars. In a room with no windows, cigar smoke would be a pain in the rear.

As he surveyed the office once more he stepped to the wall and adjusted the tilt of the framed document hanging there. He'd worked damn hard for that piece of paper and the right to add CPA after his signature. How easily would an accountant mesh with a guy who ran a business called Fancy Footwork?

The office they would share was anything but fancy. It contained two desks, four chairs—his, Dugan's, and two for clients—and a polished brass coatrack. That was it, except for the framed document and one painting. He'd allowed himself the luxury of buying the seascape of waves crashing on Waikiki beach. After all, there had been some good in those crazy years. One very good thing in particular.

And tomorrow Riley Dugan would arrive, providing just the financial boost he needed. Banning turned on his answering machine, flipped off the lights, and left the office, locking the door carefully behind him.

With a cry of triumph Riley located the correct number of the office. Her arm ached from holding the macramé hanger supporting the spider plant. Juggling the staghorn fern to the crook of her left arm, she opened the door and walked in.

"Mr. Scott?"

He stood up immediately and rounded the desk. Tall, Riley thought. And nice shoulders. Capable-looking.

12

"Can I help you with something?" he asked with polite concern. "Those plants . . ."

"Are for this office," she said, completing his sentence.

"I don't understand."

He seemed so poised, so in charge of the situation, that Riley almost hated to disrupt his confident manner. But he had to find out sometime. "I'm Riley Dugan." She ignored the weight of the hanging pot and watched his reaction. She'd looked forward to this fun little surprise all the way to Seattle.

"I . . . you . . ." He wasn't laughing, as she had thought he might. Instead, he looked as if someone had spilled motor oil on his conservative gray suit.

"I'm glad to meet you, Mr. Scott," she said, curbing her own impulse to laugh. She was very glad to meet him. She'd hoped for nice, courteous, honest, but she hadn't dared hope for handsome too. The luck of the Irish must have followed her across the country.

"I'm . . . glad to meet you, Miss Dugan." A woman? Riley Dugan was a woman? All his preconceived notions tumbled into disarray.

"I need to put this somewhere before my arm falls off." She glanced around the room and spied the brass coatrack. "There!" She hurried over and suspended the plant from a shiny hook. "Poor baby. You've had a rough trip, but we'll have you fixed up in a jiffy. Just wait here."

Banning winced as the pot clattered against the

13

side of the polished brass. *Wait here?* Where was the bedraggled thing going?

"And you, Methuselah, need to be hung on the wall right away. We can find the perfect spot later."

Banning opened his mouth as she headed straight for his CPA certificate and lifted it from the nail. Then he closed his mouth again. Maybe this was a dream he was having. Or a nightmare.

Sure enough, this Riley Dugan, this woman, had put his certificate on the floor and replaced it with a hunk of wood about the size and shape of deer antlers with some mossy stuff growing out of it like a green beard. No pot or anything to hold water.

"Now for the other one," she said, turning toward the brass coatrack again. "How about a nice northern exposure for a while, sweetheart? Then we can move you if—my God, there aren't any windows in this place!"

"Miss Dugan, I think we need to have a—"

"Oh, call me Riley, please. After all, we're going to be office partners. May I call you Banning?"

"I guess so, but shouldn't we—"

"I certainly expected windows. Don't you feel claustrophobic not being able to see out?"

"No. I'm too busy working and it rains a lot in Seattle. Besides, the inside offices are cheaper."

"I'm sure they are, but wouldn't a window be worth the extra expense?"

"I didn't think so when I rented the office space." He discovered he was clenching both hands. This was not the Riley Dugan he expected.

And this Riley Dugan looked like more trouble than he had bargained for. "Perhaps you'd like to locate another—"

"Oh, no! I couldn't go through all that again. I'll manage somehow. Grow lights for the plants, I suppose, and maybe even one for me." She laughed and returned her attention to the partially crushed spider plant.

He stared at her while she crooned over the bent leaves. Maybe she did need a grow light. She reminded him of some exotic flower, with her curly mass of dark hair and the red jacket that came to mid-thigh. Her slim black skirt appeared conservative at first, until she walked and revealed the slit that went all the way to the hem of her jacket.

"Do you have some scissors, Banning?"

"Scissors." Still thinking about the slit in her skirt, he went automatically to his top desk drawer and took out the requested item. So Riley Dugan was a woman. A woman who fussed over wilting plants. And had terrific legs. What now?

Maybe having a woman in the office wouldn't be so bad. She probably didn't smoke cigars, and what did a couple of plants matter? He'd move the bearded one somewhere else, and they'd hang the other one up by her desk. No big deal. He handed her the scissors.

"Thanks. My patient needs immediate surgery." Bending and turning, giving him several opportunities to further assess her legs, Riley snipped away at the plant dangling from his brass coatrack.

"My poor sweetheart," she said, working with Banning's scissors until the plant was reduced to a few pale leaves hanging limply from the edge of the pot. "You're in shock, aren't you, Spidey? And I'm not surprised, after that long, nasty trip. Now you can relax and adjust to your new home. Settle in and concentrate on getting well. Then you can start having more babies."

Banning massaged his temples. Did she say babies? He could have sworn she did. Then he watched with horror as she used the scissors to poke vigorously through the dirt around the plant.

"There, doesn't that feel better? Loosen up and stretch out. We made it, and we're here to stay." Riley started to hand him the scissors and then drew them back. "I got your scissors a little dirty."

"Did you? I hadn't noticed." He glanced pointedly at his cherished carpet strewn with brown stems. "Maybe I was too busy thinking about the rug."

"I'll take care of that right away." She stooped and gathered up the dry stalks. "Wastebasket?"

Banning cleared his throat. "Over there by your desk." When she had crouched down to pick up the plant pieces, he'd gotten an eyeful of those nonstop legs. Oh, well, what was a little dirt and plant juice on his scissors and debris on his carpet?

She stuffed the mess into her wastebasket and handed him the dirty scissors. "Thanks," she said with relief, dusting off her hands. "Now, where shall we put this thing?" She gestured toward the laminated desk.

"You don't need a desk?"

"Of course I do, but not there, all lined up precisely with yours. Looks like we're in the military." She gave him a bright smile and turned her head from side to side, deciding.

Banning figured he needed to take control of the situation, and soon, but everything about her distracted him, from her large hoop earrings that flashed when she moved her head to the three-inch black heels that made her legs look like they went on forever.

"I think maybe on an angle, over there," she said, crossing to the desk and starting to drag it across the carpet.

"Wait! The phone cord won't reach." He grabbed the black instrument before the cord snapped.

"Oh." She considered for a moment before waving her hand dismissively. "I can buy an extension for the cord. No problem." She started to drag the desk once more.

"Hold it. I'll help." To save the carpet, he plopped the phone on the floor and dashed to the other end of the desk. "Can you lift it up a little?"

"Sure."

They hoisted the desk a few inches from the floor and stood facing each other. For the first time Banning looked directly into her eyes. Green. Of course with a name like Riley Dugan, her eyes would be that color.

"Which way?" he asked.

"If you go to your left and back, I'll come around to my left." She indicated the directions with a slight movement of her head, and the earrings glittered golden against her dark hair.

They shuffled around until the desk was at a forty-five-degree angle from his.

"Okay," she said, breathing a little harder. "Now forward a little. To the right. No, too far. Let's set it down for a minute." She walked to the front of the office and put one finger against her lips as she contemplated. "Not quite right. The angle is okay, but the desk should be on the other side of the room."

"What about the telephone?"

Riley laughed. "More extension cords." She returned to her end of the desk as if there could be no doubt that Banning would help her again. And he did.

"Around this way," Riley directed, tossing her head toward the opposite wall. "A little more. Back that way. There. Perfect."

Banning set down his end of the desk and took out his handkerchief to wipe his hands. The arrangement looked ridiculous, but he appreciated the way her chest rose and fell from the exertion of the move. "You like it like that, all catawampus?" he asked, straightening his tie.

"Yep." She placed both hands on her hips and smiled with satisfaction. "Much better. Would you like to turn yours that way now? Or maybe the opposite angle, so that we'd have even more interesting—"

"No, thanks." Banning moved back to his desk in a quick, protective gesture. "Besides, mine's too heavy to cart around, even for two people."

"I noticed the wood. Nice."

He wondered if she was disappointed with her

own laminated desk, then chastised himself for caring. She had a desk, didn't she? And a chair, and good carpeting. She could damn well be content with that.

Riley sighed. "They couldn't cut a window in this wall over here, could they? I'm so used to looking out."

"If they cut a window in that wall, you'd have a nice view of Thelma, the secretary for the real estate office next door."

"Oh. I guess you're right. Then maybe in the back?"

"None of these are outside walls, Riley. Otherwise we would have a window. As I said before, that's why the rent is—"

"I know. Cheaper. And Lord knows I can't afford anything more expensive than this right now. But someday, Banning, I intend to have a floor-to-ceiling window overlooking Puget Sound!" She spread her arms wide and twirled in the middle of the room.

"I hope you do." Something told him that despite her obvious physical charms, this woman prancing around his office was going to be more bother than he ever imagined. But he needed her rent money. Needed it desperately.

He cringed at asking the next question, but he was too much of a gentleman not to. "Do you have, uh, anything else to move in?"

"Just a few boxes. You know, my calculator and stuff. Can't live without my calculator. I'll bet you're that way too. If you wouldn't mind helping me with them, that would be great. Then I'll get

Cyclops and be off. I still have a million things to do at the apartment."

She was out the door and hurrying down the two flights of stairs to the main floor before he had a chance to ask who the hell Cyclops was. He wouldn't be surprised if she had a one-eyed horse to move in also. Quickly turning on the answering machine, Banning followed her, taking the steps two at a time.

Riley pulled the van's keys from the pocket of her jacket as she crossed the parking lot. She sensed she'd gotten off on the wrong foot with Banning Scott. Maybe he didn't like plants as much as she did.

Come to think of it, there hadn't been a single one in the room until she arrived. How could he work in that office without plants, without a window, with one measly picture on the wall?

She probably shouldn't have let Banning believe she was a man, either. Riley knew that now, after seeing his no-nonsense approach. She had expected, hoped, they'd share a good laugh over the whole incident. Instead, Banning kept staring at her as if she were a creature from another planet.

For her part, Riley found it difficult to avoid staring back at him. She admired his high forehead, his freshly shaven square chin, and his ears. Riley always noticed ears, and his were definitely the kind she'd like to nibble on.

Riley wondered if Banning Scott liked to have his ears nibbled. It would be easy to do, because he wore his brown hair cut short, like an athlete's. A faint sun streak ran through it, and Riley tried to imagine him cavorting around outdoors. In his gray suit and dark striped tie, he seemed very much the indoorsy, serious businessman.

She heard his footsteps behind her and walked faster. Her best plan was to get the boxes moved upstairs and leave before any other incidents marred this first meeting.

Did he mind that she changed the position of the desk? Certainly he could see that lining them up like rows of Iowa corn was so unimaginative.

She fit the key in the back double door of the red van. *Fancy Footwork* curled in elaborate gold script across the doors and on each side of the van. Just looking at the classy logo gave Riley more confidence.

"Who or what is Cyclops?"

"Oh, Banning, there you are." She turned as if surprised to see him standing beside her. "Cyclops?" She swung the doors wide. "Ta-da!"

"A motorcycle?"

"My saving grace." Riley patted the glossy black fender. "A million miles to the gallon."

"You ride this?"

"Sure. All the time. In fact, I plan to leave the van parked here and use the cycle to get back and forth to work." She reached for the catch on the metal ramp. "I'll back this baby out of here first, so we can get to the boxes."

"Let me help you." He stepped forward.

"No, no. I'm used to this. If you can just steady it, I'll take care of the rest." She hiked up her skirt and used the ramp to climb into the van. "Cyclops and I have learned to maneuver in tight spots, haven't we, buddy?" Riley released the kickstand and nudged the cycle backward until it began rolling down the ramp.

Banning laid a hand on the seat and kept the cycle from falling while Riley hopped down. The supple leather warmed under his touch and he was engulfed with memories of windswept rides beneath a tropical sun.

"I've got it," she said, grasping the handlebar on her side.

He released his hold reluctantly. While she parked the cycle he turned and peered into the unusual interior of the van.

"Come on, I'll give you a tour of my traveling shoe store." Riley mounted the ramp again and rolled up the rubber mat that had cushioned the cycle's tires.

Her new office partner had to be impressed with her setup in here, she decided. Maybe a withering spider plant hadn't been her best introduction, but this van was wonderful. Jordan's money had been good for something. It hadn't salvaged their marriage, but it had launched her business in fine style.

Banning followed her into the van. "It looks like a shoe store, all right," he admitted, surveying the slanted display shelves that ran from waist-high to the ceiling along each wall. One side was devoted to women's shoes and the other to men's. Below the mirror-backed shelves were cupboards, and two upholstered chairs were bolted into the front portion of the van just behind the driver's seat. He walked to the rack of men's shoes, picked up a soft gray loafer and flexed the sole.

"Like that style? I might have your size."

Banning put the shoe back immediately. "No, that's okay. I didn't mean—I was curious, that's all."

"Don't be silly. Sit down and let me measure your foot. I think a complimentary pair of shoes would be a fine way to begin this liaison."

"Liaison?"

Riley laughed. "I mean partnership. Working relationship . . . whatever. Come on, sit down. I'll demonstrate my sales technique for you. Don't you want to know if I'll be successful or not? You can't tell unless you see my sales approach."

She expected his hesitation, but she was betting on something else she suspected might lurk behind that reserve. A hint of sensuality had flickered across his face when they lifted the desk together and were forced to concentrate on each other.

Banning shrugged and sat down. "As long as we're out here, why not?"

"That's the spirit!" Riley stepped between the two chairs, brushing against his jacket sleeve in the process, and flipped a switch on the van's overhead panel. "Lights, camera, action!"

He blinked at the dazzling array of tiny bulbs that flashed on around each set of shelves and reflected in the mirrors behind them. "Won't you run down the battery?"

"Nope. I'm set up for this." She touched a button and low-pitched music wafted from speakers in the front and back of the van. "To get the full effect, we have to close the doors." Sliding between the chairs again, Riley was very aware of her hip touching his elbow. He didn't move to give her more room.

Riley pulled the doors closed with a solid thud and turned to find him looking at her the same way he had when they were moving the desk. And she kind of liked his expression.

"Well, Mr. Scott," she began, rubbing her hands together, "I'm here to save you time and money. Busy men like you haven't the time to tramp through shopping malls in search of quality footwear. My service brings the shoe store to you, at your convenience. The samples you see on my shelves are only the tip of the iceberg. I have a complete catalog for your examination as well."

Banning raised one eyebrow in approval. "I'm impressed."

"If you're impressed by the selection, Mr. Scott, you'll be even more pleased with the comfort of my shoes. At Fancy Footwork we have a no-blister policy."

"Oh, really?" The beginning of a smile played around his lips.

"Absolutely." She sensed that he was mellowing. "If your shoes give you blisters, you may demand another shoe or a full refund."

"And if the next shoe rubs more blisters?"

Riley made a mental note. This was an exacting man. "Then we'll keep working until we find the shoe that fits. Let me see what size we're dealing with."

She took a folding stool and her wooden measuring stick from a cupboard. The stool had been specially made for her and resembled those used in shoe stores. "Put your left foot up here, please."

Banning followed her instructions.

As she loosened the laces of his black oxford, Riley wished her hands would stop their trembling. Maybe Banning hadn't noticed, but she had, and that was almost as bad. She'd sat like this at the feet of countless businessmen, and she'd always been cool as a cucumber. If she didn't get herself together, Banning might think she was a bumbling idiot at this job.

Grasping the heel of his shoe, she slid it from his foot with one hand and cradled his instep in her other palm. The warmth of his skin, penetrating the gray dress sock, tingled through her hand and up her arm. Could she do this? He was very close, close enough that she could smell his skin and the scent of his soap.

Instinctively she glanced up and found Banning watching her with a glow of sensuality playing hide-and-seek in his expression. She released his foot.

"Stand with your toe against this crosspiece, please, Mr. Scott." Silently he complied, and she finished the measurement quickly. "Size eleven, D width. I should have the gray loafer in that size. If you'll have a seat again, I'll check."

With great relief she leapt up and began rummaging through the cupboards. "Ah-ha. Here we are." Taking her shoehorn from its hook on the wall, Riley returned with the rectangular box and took the left shoe out of the tissue paper. Sitting once more at Banning's feet, she eased the soft loafer on.

"That's some shoehorn," he commented.

"My, uh, financial backer thought I should have a gold-plated one."

"With a walnut handle, no less."

"Fancy Footwork's customers need to feel pampered. That's part of the appeal."

"I see."

"How does the shoe fit, Mr. Scott?"

"Not bad."

"Would you like to try the other one?"

"Sure."

Riley noted the antagonism was gone from his voice. Had she scored a victory with this pair of shoes? It wouldn't be the first time she saw somebody's mood improve after putting on more comfortable footwear.

Because of her physical reaction to his nearness, she steeled herself against the necessary contact with him as she removed his other shoe and replaced it with the loafer. After all, that was part of the service. Fancy Footwork customers didn't try on their own shoes. But the sensation of touching him again destroyed her composure.

"You should walk around in them," she advised in a shaky voice, and scooted her stool back to give him room to get up.

"Okay." He paced the length of the van. "I must admit they're the most comfortable shoes I've ever had on."

"They're yours." She admired the fluid motion of his walk. Where had he developed such ease of movement? Surely not sitting behind a desk eight hours a day.

"Oh, no. I'll pay for them. You've got a business to run."

Riley put his black oxfords in the empty shoe box. "And you've provided a place from which to run it. Take the shoes, please." She was delighted that she'd made a hit. She'd win this man over yet. "Now I'd better get my supplies up to the office. If you'll open the back doors again, I'll get the most important boxes."

Riley shut off the music and the lights before hefting one of several cardboard boxes stacked next to the driver's seat. "This should go first. Has my calculator and desk supplies." She walked to the back of the van and set the box down.

"I'll take that." Banning put his shoe box on top of the carton and lifted them both together.

"Thanks. I'll get one more and we'll go up."

"By the way, the building does have an elevator."

"For two flights? I wouldn't dream of using it. The exercise is great for the calf muscles. Let's see —I guess this one is next most important." She returned with another box.

"I can take that one, too, and you can bring the third and save another trip."

"That would be great." Riley moved the shoe box and plopped the second carton on top of the first.

"Ooff! What's in that one?"

"Oh, lots of things." Riley crowned his pile with

the shoe box. "Plant food, a watering can, and of course my snacks."

"Snacks?" His voice was muffled by the boxes, which reached to his nose.

"Oh, you know, the usual—crackers, peanut butter, trail mix."

When her explanation was met with silence she shot him a furtive glance. All she could see above the boxes were his eyes and his furrowed brow. His eyes reminded her of the ocean pictured on his wall, blue and stormy. What had she done wrong now? "Don't you like trail mix?" she asked hesitantly.

"I usually don't eat while I'm working."

There it was again, the disapproving tone. She gritted her teeth. How could such a young, good-looking guy be such a stick-in-the-mud? Maybe he needed her influence to put some zing in his life. "You'd be surprised how a little handful of trail mix boosts your energy," she said, going back for the last box.

"Riley, I think there are a few things we should—"

She didn't want to hear it. Evasive action was called for. "Oh, my God, look at the time! I'm supposed to be home for the telephone people. Banning, could you run those two boxes up for me? I'll just lock the van and be off. I can bring the last box later."

"But we haven't talked about—"

"Later. We'll settle everything later." She had the ramp back in place and the van locked in no time. "Thanks for taking the boxes. See you later."

With lightning speed she strapped on her helmet, pulled her skirt up to her thighs, and jumped on the cycle.

Banning stood and watched her career out of the parking lot, her red jacket flapping in the wind. This wasn't going to work and he needed to tell her so. But she had successfully escaped, on a cycle for God's sake, and left him holding her trail mix and peanut butter. However, when she came back he would explain that their personalities were not compatible.

And then he remembered the note that had arrived in this morning's mail—the note from Zabrina. She was counting the days until she could see him. While she counted days, he counted dollars, wanting so much to show her a good time. Riley Dugan represented a good hunk of those dollars. He might as well learn to tolerate her—trail mix, wilted plants, furniture arranging and all.

CHAPTER TWO

"G'morning, Brit! I want you to know I made a special effort to get up early so I could call before eight, when it's cheaper."

"Riley! I'm so glad to hear from you. Watching your pennies now, huh? How was your trip?"

"It was fine. Gee, you sound so close, Brit, not all the way across the country."

"Miracles of modern science, Riley. How do you like the West Coast?"

"It's beautiful out here. You should see my apartment. I have a teeny-tiny balcony, and if you stand at the very end and lean to the right, you can see Puget Sound! You'd be so proud of how neat everything is in here, Brit. That's because my furniture hasn't arrived yet so the place is nearly empty. But I got a terrific bargain on the new furniture. I get to use it now but don't have to pay until later."

"Sounds like your kind of deal, Riley," Brit said, laughing. "And a lovely apartment."

"Who was that fabulous voice who answered the phone? Do you have a new French maid?" Riley asked.

"No, of course not," Brit said. "I programmed the robot that answers the phone to have a French accent. Got the idea from you, Riley, when you came to help me serve that first night I met Harrison. Remember that?"

"Oh, yes. Speaking of your handsome hubby, how are things going with your new family?" Riley shifted the phone to the other ear and sipped her morning tea.

"Wonderful. The kids are busy with summer projects, Harrison has a new invention going, and my business is better than ever. Including the new robot in The Quintessential Woman was a stroke of genius. I've doubled my volume and halved my staff."

"Now you're talking out of my range, like the businesswoman you are, Brit. Wish you were here to help me get started. Boy, do I miss you."

"Trouble getting Fancy Footwork on its feet? Maybe I can give you a few pointers over the phone."

"It's about the office. My partner is kind of quiet and reserved. We don't exactly mesh."

"Let me guess—the Woody Allen type?"

Riley paused and considered the ludicrous comparison. "Not at all, Brit. He's real, uh, well, quite a hunk, with beautiful blue eyes, brown hair with light streaks, and he's about six feet tall—"

"Riley—"

"He's a CPA, sort of conservative, brilliant with figures."

"Sounds like my kind of guy," Brit admitted

31

with a happy lilt to her voice. "So what's the prob?"

Riley sighed. "I think the problem's me. I've been there three days now and—"

"You haven't had an argument already, have you?"

"No. But sometimes he looks at me funny. Just watches me with a strange expression in his eyes, you know? I think he doesn't like me."

"I'm sure that's not it, Riley," Brit answered quickly. "I'd say he's just having trouble getting used to all the, uh, changes now that he's sharing an office. You didn't move in like gangbusters, did you?"

"All I did was hang a couple of plants," Riley explained. "And I had to install a grow light. But that's because the stupid office has no windows and you know how I *need* natural light."

"Yes, I know. Which plants?"

"The spider and the staghorn fern. Poor Spidey didn't make the trip very well. I had to trim him right down to the nub when I got him here. You know, Brit, I don't understand how anyone could tolerate an office with no windows. Then I fixed the desk better. The place looked like a military camp with everything just so. And I—"

"Look, Riley, please take it easy for a while. No more changes. Give the man time to adjust . . . er, to get to know you and understand you a little better. Don't push too much too soon."

"Maybe you're right, Brit. I will—uh-oh! It's time for my big delivery!"

"The new furniture?"

"No, that's next week. Today I'm getting a big shipment at the office. Plus, I have to pick up my new phone on the way. It's smashing! I can't wait till Banning sees it! I hope he likes it. Well, gotta go, Brit. Thanks for the advice. I'll slow down. Because I do want him to like me."

"After your description of him, I can imagine why."

"Oh, it's nothing like that, Brit. He's so businesslike. But I do want a friendly office. Well, ta-ta! Have a good time today!"

"You, too, Riley. Great to talk to you." Brit hung up the phone with a wistful feeling deep inside. Riley didn't have to be reminded to have a good time today. She did it anyway, because that's the way she was.

"Hi, darling. Have you got a minute?"

Brit looked up and smiled at her husband. He looked so handsome with his hair slightly tousled and his shirt sleeves rolled up. "Time for you, Harrison? Always. That was Riley on the phone, all the way from Seattle."

"Oh? How is she?"

Brit smiled wickedly. "Riley's fine. The question of the day is 'How is her office partner faring?' "

"She taking the place by storm?"

"You might say that." Brit nodded. "But what's new? So what are you up to, honey?"

He looked at her expectantly. "I want to show you something. Now, remember, it's still in the preliminary stages. . . ." Harrison slipped his arm around his wife's shoulders and steered her toward the workshop.

"I'd love to see it." Brit McIver Kent fell into step with him, her arm curling naturally around his waist. She had never been so happy—or so in love—in her life and knew she was probably the luckiest woman alive to have such a fantastic and bright husband. And such a beautiful little family with Harrison's three kids. She could only hope the same for her friend Riley someday.

"Where should I put these boxes?"

"What boxes?"

"These boxes." A heavyset, uniformed delivery-man entered the office steering a dolly loaded to the top with small, oblong boxes.

"What's that?" Banning Scott glared at the uni-formed deliveryman, his sharp eyes noting the en-signia on the man's front pocket. "I didn't order anything from your company, sir."

The man propped the dolly against his substan-tial chest while he checked the order form in his shirt pocket. "Says here, Suite 314, Emerson Title and Trust Building." He glanced back at the door for assurance. "Yep. This is it."

"But what—"

"Shoes."

"Huh? Shoes?" By now Banning was on his feet. *Shoes, of course. His wonderful office partner!* "Oh, they must be for—"

"Something called Fancy Footwork. Riley Du-gan."

Banning nodded toward the angled desk. "Yes, that's my, uh, they belong at that desk. And, as you can see, Riley Dugan isn't here yet."

"Don't matter. You can sign." He waved the order blank at Banning.

"I will not! That's not my function around here."

"Look, mister, I got work to do. I ain't got time to wait around till some loafer gets to work. You don't have to pay the bill here. Just sign that you received this shipment at this address. He'll be billed later."

"He?" Banning frowned. "Oh, you mean Riley. She. Riley's a woman."

"Oh, well, whatever. Sign this while I get started. Got a boatload of 'um to haul up here."

Banning's pen poised over the line on the order form. "How many?" he asked, but he dreaded to hear the answer.

The deliveryman expertly shoved the dolly's load into the corner. "A hundred and ten."

"A hundred and ten?" Banning's voice exploded. "Where the hell are you going to put a hundred shoe boxes in here?"

After a quick glance around the office, the deliveryman nodded reassuringly. "Not to worry. They'll all fit."

Banning examined the floor space, trying to imagine how a hundred shoe boxes would add to the clutter already in the office. A hundred *and ten* boxes.

Soon he stared at a hundred and ten shoe boxes, two straggly hanging plants, and a potted tree beside the angled desk, an extra table containing a hot plate and a small, square refrigerator—all belonging to one Riley Dugan.

In that instant he decided that today they would have it out. Not one day longer.

He'd let her flit in and out for three days. They hadn't even signed the office agreement he'd so carefully worked out. Banning shook his head and rubbed his face with large, frustrated hands. Maybe they shouldn't sign any agreement at all. What the hell was he getting himself into with this Riley Dugan? If he didn't need her contributions, absolutely *need* her, he'd drop the whole thing and struggle on alone.

No. He'd made a commitment, even if only verbally. Banning Scott was as good as his word and he would stand by it. Thank God he'd listed the time limit of the office agreement as one year; then they'd renegotiate. *But could he stand one full year of Riley Dugan?*

Riley wheeled Cyclops into the office parking lot and checked her watch. A little late. Oh, well. Couldn't be perfect. Thank goodness Banning was there to receive her shipment. She grabbed her new phone and practically ran inside.

"Hi!" She grinned happily at Banning, then turned to admire the stacks of shoe boxes. "I see they made it. Wow! How exciting!"

"Yes, that's what I said," Banning muttered coolly.

"Did you have to sign?"

"There was no one else." His expression was impassive.

"Gee, thanks." Riley tucked her phone into the crook of her arm. "You know that's one of the good

36

things about having an office partner. You can do things for each other."

"One of them." *And sharing expenses. That's about it.* He eyed the orange and black contraption in her arm, but resisted asking about it. He might not like the answer.

Riley walked around the stacks of shoe boxes, trying to find her desk. "Wow, this is a lot, isn't it? Did they deliver them all?"

"All one hundred and ten."

Her green eyes lit up. "Did you count them?"

"Didn't have to. The deliveryman enumerated."

She nodded with satisfaction. "This is great."

"That's what I said," Banning repeated in a cold tone. "Great. This is just great."

She looked up at him, startled. "What's wrong?"

Banning stood up and knotted his fists, trying to control his tone of voice. And his temper. "Well, Miss Dugan, I can't help wondering—what next?"

"Riley. Call me Riley. Surely we're good enough friends by now to call each other by first names."

"Friends? I just want us to be amiable office partners. Friends go into another category altogether."

She blinked. He was definitely unhappy and she'd better do something quick. But what? "Look, Banning, I can explain about these—"

"I hope so. Because I want some answers. Like where do you intend to put all these shoe boxes? They must be stored somewhere!"

"Can't they stay where they are until they're sold?"

"Until they're sold? You mean they aren't sold yet? Then why . . . how . . . ?"

She shook her head honestly. "The manufacturer ran a special on a terrific little sport shoe. And if I ordered a hundred, I got ten pairs free. I figured it would only be a matter of time until—"

He slapped his palm to his forehead. "You mean you ordered all these just to get ten free pairs? And they aren't even sold? My God, you aren't established in Seattle yet. That's poor business practice, you know."

Her eyes widened. "I thought it was a good business move. Free shoes mean more profit in my book, Mr. Scott."

"*If* you sell them. Until then you're using this office as a warehouse? It looks like a shoe mountain over there. You can't leave them. Why, I have clients—"

"Tell them I'll give them a bargain price on a pair of sport shoes," she offered with a sassy grin.

"I'm sorry, they can't stay here."

"Please, Banning. I'll sell them in no time. Honest. Come on, loosen up. I'll haul them to the back. We have that storage room."

"Small storage room."

"Well . . ." She shrugged. "I'll think of something. Meantime, I guess I'd better get to work."

"Riley, we have some things to discuss. Like the preoccupancy agreement."

"Pre- *what?*"

He whipped out three copies of neatly typed pages. "Why don't you have a seat and we'll go over this list? Just so we understand it and agree. And sign."

"Is this like a prenuptial agreement?" she asked, her green eyes dancing.

He nodded curtly, refusing to give in to her humor. "It pertains only to the office we'll be sharing. But it's the same idea."

"Okay." She pulled her chair around to his desk and his gaze caught the trail the chair legs left on the new carpet. "Show me," she said, cradling the orange and black item in her arms.

Banning glanced down and could see it was a plastic cat. *A cat?* He didn't dare ask. "Number one is office rent, including insurance. You pay this amount. And if you default . . . et cetera." He tried to ignore her shapely legs and the slender, glamorous feet arched by her high-heeled shoes. He cleared his throat. "Number two has to do with utilities. Water, electricity, cleaning fees, phones—"

"Oh, I don't have to worry about that part." She picked up a pen and quickly crossed off "telephone rental." "I brought my own phone."

"You'll still have the monthly fee for the line."

She proudly plopped the orange and black cat on the desk and lifted its tail to reveal the touchtone dialing system. "This is Garfield. His eyes open when you lift the receiver. Isn't he cute?"

Banning's gaze riveted to the cat-phone. "This is your business phone?"

"Why not? Livens up the place, don't you think? Especially when his eyes open." She angled her head and studied the cat. "I considered Kermit the Frog, but I'm glad I picked this one. I like Garfield much better, don't you?"

"What's wrong with the one on your desk?" Banning felt himself going stiff all over. This woman was impossible.

Riley wrinkled her nose. "That old black thing? You expect me to poke my finger in those tiny holes and *dial?* I already broke a fingernail. See? And it just ruins your polish."

"I never considered your nails." His glance went to both her hands and he had to admit they were graceful and quite pretty. The fingers were long and tapered and the nails were perfect ovals, painted shiny red. They probably never did a drop of real work, other than fitting men's shoes. He remembered how those slender hands felt on his own feet when she stroked his arch—

"My hands must make a nice appearance in my work. Surely you understand." She held them out for further perusal.

"Well, yes, I can see it would ruin, uh, I can understand your reluctance to poke your finger, uh . . ." He cleared his throat and proceeded. "Number three on the agreement deals with . . ."

Banning read the entire page to her, regretting he hadn't had the forethought to add something about the office being used as a storage room for a hundred and ten shoe boxes. But Riley was so sweet and agreeable to everything listed on the page, he felt he had accomplished a lot in getting her signature on it.

Except for the phone. Her desk was now the home of Garfield, whose eyes opened whenever she lifted the tail. And perhaps she was right. The strange-looking phone livened up the place . . . if one considered that the place needed livening now that Riley Dugan was on the scene.

Although Banning found himself looking forward to each succeeding day with a sense of anticipation of what Riley would do next, the rest of the week was rather uneventful. The only thing Riley added was an oriental silk brocade folding screen to hide the shoe boxes. It concealed about half of them. But the screen was obviously expensive and quite attractive, and it served to liven up the place even more.

By the end of the second week Banning and Riley were falling into a pattern and adjusting to each other's quirks and habits. Or, rather, Banning was adjusting. On Friday night they both found themselves working late. It was something Banning accepted as a routine part of self-employment but one that Riley abhorred. She didn't try to hide her feelings.

"Darn! What a waste of a perfectly good night!" Riley spritzed the leaves of her plants and paused to murmur something affectionate to each one. "Oh, Spidey, you're looking so much healthier, sweetheart. And Methuselah, I bet you're glad *you* don't have sales reports to fill out." Then she stashed the squirt bottle and took more time adjusting the silk screen around the pile of shoes.

Banning watched her with amusement. "Pardon me for saying so, but if you'd get to your business, you'd be finished faster and you wouldn't have to waste a perfectly good night."

She glared at him. "You sound like my father."

"Your father must be a very wise man," he observed.

"Yes, as a matter of fact, he was."

"Was?"

"He died a couple of years ago, shortly after we lost the family farm."

"I'm sorry, Riley." Banning leaned forward on his desk with a sincere look on his face. "That must have been very traumatic for you and your family."

"It was." She circled her desk and pinched a drooping leaf from a nearby plant. "And I meant it as a compliment when I said you sound like him, Banning. He just happened to choose a losing profession."

"Is that why you decided to go into shoes?"

"One of the reasons. I figured everybody always needs shoes, even in bad times. But my concept of taking the product to the customer, especially the busy executive customer, is unique. And I expect it to be successful."

"So do I." Banning smiled at the perky brunette, who was still delaying sitting at her desk. "Actually, Riley, I think the concept for Fancy Footwork is very wise. Sounds to me like you're very much your father's daughter."

She beamed at him, then sighed. "I guess you and my father are right. I'd better get to work if I ever expect to get finished tonight." Finally she sat down, tuned the portable radio, and hauled out her calculator. "This is the part I hate most. Trying to make the columns add up."

She continued to mumble to herself for a while and Banning continued to ignore her. Or tried to.

She was so damn cute, with her legs curled up in the chair and her shoes kicked aside. They weren't exactly shoes—some kind of blue, soft leather boots. She wore a lightweight sweater and had shoved the sleeves up past her elbows. Her hair became a tousled cap of curls as she ran frustrated fingers through it. Banning found himself more intrigued with watching her antics than finishing his own work.

He glanced at his watch. Damn! Already late! He needed to call Gwyn soon and let her know he was still working and they'd have to have a late supper. She'd be furious, but what the hell? She should be used to it by now.

His gaze roamed over to Riley, who was becoming more and more agitated by the moment. And more appealing to his senses. At that moment he realized that he hadn't told Gwyn that Riley Dugan was a female. Or anything about his new office partner. Well, it didn't matter because—

"Oooh, no!" Riley moaned aloud. "Not again! I just changed the battery and it's out of juice already. Now I absolutely can't function! Maybe I can get another. What time is it?"

"Nine-o-four."

"Drat! Stores are closed." With an audible wail she shoved the inept calculator aside and covered her face with her hands. "I need more than a battery to straighten up this mess. I'll never get my report in the mail in time. It screws up everything.

Now I won't get my check in time to pay any of my bills!"

Banning's head shot up and his interest increased tenfold. "Can I help?"

She lowered her hands and he could see the frustration in her face . . . and tears in her green eyes. Oh God, he had to help. This definitely would not do. He couldn't leave his office partner in tears.

"C-could you help me?"

"Well, I'm not exactly a wizard, but I do have a way with figures and a working calculator."

"Oh, Banning, I would be so grateful if you'd help me with this little bit. It's the only part of my job I hate. I love the people part and the shoe part and even fitting shoes on people's feet. But adding and subtracting have always been the bane of my existence. And I . . . just . . . can't make it work right." A tear rolled down her adorable cheek and his heart melted a little.

He grabbed his calculator and rolled his chair over to her desk, oblivious to the marks it made on the carpet. "Let's see what you have here."

"This page must coincide with this page." She began riffling through the papers on her desk. "And these are the totals of my sales this week. They just don't add up."

He reached for the portable radio on the desk and clicked it off. "Do you mind? We need a little peace and quiet to concentrate here."

She grinned. "It's an old habit of mine. Maybe it isn't such a good one."

"Not for me, anyway," he murmured, then tore

44

his gaze from her face and down to the dull figures scribbled on the papers. "Are these all the sales? Any from the previous week?"

"No," she said firmly. "This is it. I sold only one pair of the free ones."

"Hmm, at that rate, this pile will be here only a hundred and nine' more weeks."

"I have a marketing strategy for them," she countered stoutly. "I just haven't had time to implement it yet. Right now I have to total all this mess each week and get it in the mail by midnight in order to get my paycheck for the week."

"We'll make your deadline by a long shot," he said confidently, and ran his finger down the column as he quickly entered the figures in his own calculator.

She noticed his large, strong hands, and with his sleeves rolled up she could see the appealing way the light hairs on his forearms curled over the muscles. The top button of his shirt was open and his tie loosened, emphasizing the width of his chest. And for a man who'd worked all day, he certainly smelled refreshing.

Riley struggled to concentrate on his efforts and not pay attention to the natural spread of his knees as he sat next to her. Occasionally his right leg brushed hers and she couldn't help thinking of him as a man—a very appealing man who was extremely smart and capable.

She watched in awe as he methodically went through all the figures and columns she showed him. He found a couple of small errors that translated into larger errors and prevented the totals being correct. But when he did them they matched perfectly. "All right, there you go," he said smoothly, with a slight grin. "They all total up. Now that wasn't so bad, was it?"

Riley looked up at him with gleaming eyes, barely resisting the urge to throw her arms around his neck. "All right! You're fantastic, Banning." She wanted to hug him out of sheer gratitude, but she didn't know how he felt about such an open display of emotions between office partners. So Riley just sat there, beaming like the cat on her desk.

"The fact that you'll get your paycheck helps us both," he said.

"How can I ever repay you?" She snapped her fingers. "How about supper? Neither of us has had a chance to eat tonight and it's after nine. What if I treat?"

"No, you don't have to—"

"But I want to, Banning. I insist."

He considered her offer. It was appealing, but what about Gwyn? When he looked into Riley's deep green eyes he couldn't bring himself to say he had a previous engagement. Something inside him snapped and suddenly Banning wanted to have a late-night supper with Riley. He'd deal with Gwyn later. "Okay, but this was no trouble, really."

"Great. I feel so much better that I can do something for you after you spent your valuable time helping me, Banning."

He wanted to drown in the green depths of her eyes and all he could think of was how absolutely beautiful she was and that he wanted to spend more time with her and find out more about this live wire who shared his office.

"Are you finished with your work?"

"Huh?" He blinked. "Finished? Oh, yes, almost. I just need to clean off my desk." Nothing he was working on was of any importance at this moment.

"Well, I need a few extra minutes to fill out this sales report listing all my totals. Uh, *your* totals. And we can go."

"Yes. That'll be fine." Banning forced himself to move away from her and resettle at his desk. Quickly he cleaned up his papers and put everything away. Then he remembered Gwyn. He picked up the phone and spoke to her in low tones.

Riley filled in the blank form and stuffed it into her order envelope. She tried to ignore the conversation Banning was having, but found it impossible. He was calling a woman and canceling an engagement tonight. And it was because of her.

Banning hung up and Riley looked sincerely at him. "I'm sorry, Banning. I didn't mean to—"

He interrupted her by holding up his hand. "You didn't. I was already late."

"And I made you even later. I didn't intend to interfere with your plans."

"If I'd wanted to keep my plans, I would have. But I'd rather go with you, Riley."

"Oh. You would?"

He looked at Riley steadily. "Sure. Gwyn is just an old friend."

"I'll bet you told her you were having dinner

47

with another old friend," Riley said with a sly smile.

"I told her I'm having dinner with my new office partner."

"Does she know your office partner is a woman?"

Banning stood up and walked around the desk. He rested his hips on the edge and assessed her frankly. "No, I haven't told Gwyn that you're an attractive female and very much a woman. Nor have I told her that I want to spend more time with you, away from the office. Now, are you ready to go, Riley?"

She nodded and stood up, her eyes large and hopeful. "Shall I drive?"

"The motorcycle?" He looked at her and a slow grin spread across his face. "Sure, why not?"

"Oh, no." Riley bit her lip. "I don't have an extra helmet."

"I do. In there." He nodded toward the small storage room.

"In there? Why?"

"Oh, it's old, and I packed it in a box of stuff I intended to give away. I just never did."

"Well, if you have a helmet, then . . ." Riley's eyes dropped to his tie. "That will have to go."

He headed for the storage room, discarding the navy- and burgundy-striped tie on the way. With a jaunty step he returned with a cardboard box crammed full of dusty old things and began sorting through it.

Riley looked on curiously. "What's that? A ukulele? Do you play?"

"Used to," he mumbled, pulling out a silver helmet and closing the box back together. Rakishly, he unbuttoned several buttons on his shirt. "How's this?"

"Better." She smiled and mentally noted the masculine swell of his chest, imagining how it would feel pressed against her back when they straddled Cyclops together. "Much better."

"I'll put the box back in the storage room," he said, and disappeared for a second.

Riley stood transfixed, watching him, noting the new, quick spring to his step . . . and the soft, gray leather loafers she had given him on his feet. He hadn't said anything about them, but he was wearing them. Maybe, just maybe, Banning Scott was softening up. A little.

CHAPTER THREE

"You've ridden on a cycle recently?" Riley couldn't imagine that he had. He seemed so staid. She glanced at his gray sedan parked a few yards away. Nice car, but very conservative.

"Once upon a time."

Riley figured a high school buddy took him for a wild ride long ago. "Then you understand how to shift your weight with the driver?"

"I think so."

"As soon as I get Cyclops started, you climb up behind me and hold on."

For dear life, Banning thought. If he had to guess, he'd say Riley drove the cycle with the same gusto she applied to everything. And who was he to judge? The Honolulu police still remembered him, no doubt.

The helmet slid over his head with easy familiarity, even though he hadn't worn it since the night Kim told him to go to hell. God, that was more than twelve years ago. He'd meant to pitch the helmet the day after he sold the cycle. But he'd kept procrastinating, for some stupid reason.

"Let's go," Riley called above the drumming engine.

Banning swung astride, settling his thighs on either side of her hips. Nice position, he decided.

"Hang on," Riley commanded.

He didn't really need to. His body had total recall of how to balance on a cycle. But he liked the idea of holding her, so he followed orders and slipped both hands beneath her cropped jacket. He could feel her warmth and his own skin began to heat.

His nose recorded a scent that reminded him of hyacinths floating on a hidden lagoon where lovers swam. "What's that perfume?" he asked.

"Obsession," she flung over her shoulder, and gunned the motor.

His grip tightened at her waist and his thighs brushed against her as they veered into Seattle's Friday-night traffic. Obsession. The word hadn't played much part in his life recently. He'd been attracted, intrigued, even satisfied with the women in his life, but never obsessed. That emotion belonged to another, more tumultuous time.

"Where to?" Riley called back to him. "I don't know the city very well yet."

He watched her shift lanes, felt the undulation of her body as she moved rhythmically with the powerful machine. She was wild, as he had predicted, but skilled. She'd hold her own on the Seattle streets.

He leaned forward and wound his arms more firmly around her waist. "I'll direct you." She fit into the circle of his embrace like the missing piece of a puzzle. "Take a left at this light." He wondered how long he could ride this way, with her enticing little rear settled into him. Not long.

"I want to take you to a nice restaurant," she said as they paused for a red light. "No hamburger joints tonight."

Banning put a little distance between them as he felt the inevitable result of her nearness threatening to give him away. "This isn't a hamburger joint. Go two blocks and take a right. It's in the middle of the next block."

"We aren't going to the same place you were taking Gwyn, are we?"

He smiled to himself. Women. "No, we're not."

"Good." She sped across the intersection.

Riley had concluded from eavesdropping on Banning's telephone call that he and Gwyn probably were lovers. Nothing specific had been said, but his tone reflected a certain intimacy that suggested more than casual dating. Riley wasn't surprised. Banning was too good-looking not to be involved with someone.

Yet despite Banning's relationship with Gwyn, he'd chosen to have dinner with his new office partner. Riley decided Gwyn must not be terribly exciting. And at that moment, with Banning's strong arms wrapped around her, Riley was glad of Gwyn's shortcomings.

Treating Banning to dinner had been an inspiration, but she hoped he'd taken her seriously about picking a nice restaurant. One that took credit cards. Otherwise, she'd be in an embarrassing situation. The cash in the purse she'd tucked into a back compartment of the cycle wouldn't buy an order of french fries.

"This is it," Banning announced.

Riley almost hated for the ride to end. Banning wasn't the first man she'd ever shared a motorcycle seat with, but he was the most perfect fit. And he'd obviously ridden a motorcycle more than once. She thought of his faintly sun-streaked hair and athletic build. What was Banning Scott really like? It would be fun finding out.

However, discovering the real Banning Scott proved tougher than she expected. Dinner was fun, but not very revealing. Somehow Banning coaxed her into tales of growing up in Iowa and the crazy dreams she and her best friend, Brit, once had. Riley explained Brit's unusual life now that she was married to an inventor with three lively children.

She omitted any mention of Jordan. Why allow a bad memory to ruin a perfectly good evening? The company was great, the food delicious, and the bill payable by credit card. As she and Banning climbed aboard Cyclops, Riley anticipated with pleasure the ride back to the office.

She wasn't disappointed. Banning nestled her securely against his broad chest and his thighs enclosed hers. His forearms around her rib cage just missed brushing the underside of her breasts, and her nerve endings seemed to hum in tune with the cycle's motor. Banning didn't say a word during the return trip, but his body spoke eloquently to her.

Too soon they reached the parking lot and Banning relinquished his hold as he swung to the pavement.

"Thanks for dinner," he said, unsnapping his helmet and lifting it off.

His hair was mussed, and Riley longed to reach out and comb it into place. Then she'd run the tip of one finger around the curve of his ear . . .

"You're welcome," she said, watching wistfully as he raked his hair back from his forehead. "Fridays have always been horrible for me, but this one was a breeze, thanks to you."

"You total your sales and send them in every Friday, then?"

"Every blasted Friday." She grimaced. "It's probably just as well. If I get so screwed up in one week, can you imagine how bollixed up I'd be in two?"

"Bollixed up," he repeated with a grin. "I haven't heard that in a while."

"One of my father's expressions. Anyway, thanks for making this Friday so pleasant."

"Anytime."

She studied him for a moment. "Do you mean that?"

"Sure."

"Because I just had a brilliant idea. Would you consider dinner every Friday in exchange for helping me with my sales report?"

Banning tucked the helmet under one arm and looked at her, considering. "I don't see why not."

"Great! Brit told me a CPA might come in handy!" Riley clapped a hand to her mouth. "My goodness, that sounded rude. I didn't mean it that way."

Wariness flickered in his blue eyes. "I'm glad my services can be of some use to you."

"Banning, please. You've adopted that formal tone again, and it's all my fault."

"Formal tone?"

"You know. When I've said or done something you don't quite approve of. My stupid statement—and I'm known to make them, believe me—sounded like I'm using you. The truth is, I'm alone in a strange city, and this is the first evening I've spent with anyone just having fun. I'd like your help with my report, but your friendship is far more important to me right now."

Slowly his expression softened. "Never let it be said that Seattle isn't a friendly town. I'll try to keep my Friday nights free from now on."

Riley remembered Gwyn. Were there others besides her? "Perhaps I'm asking too much, intruding on your social life like that. I'm not sure that Gwyn will under—"

"It doesn't matter."

"It doesn't?"

He held her gaze. "No."

Riley started the motorcycle. "Then I'll see you on Monday." She churned out of the parking lot, afraid if she stayed any longer he'd see the triumph in her expression. Gwyn didn't matter!

If Riley used to dread Fridays, now the day couldn't come fast enough. True to his word, Banning stacked his own work in a neat pile at five o'clock and brought his chair and adding machine over to her desk once more.

"I've replaced the batteries," she said, offering him her portable calculator.

"We might as well use this and save your batteries for another time," he said, reaching behind her to plug in his machine. "Why don't you get one that runs on regular current? It would be cheaper in the long run."

"Because I couldn't take it with me in the van and add anywhere I wanted to. I shouldn't have to be concerned with math when I'm working with a customer, so I need the calculator then."

"But it's only a simple—"

"So it's not simple for me, okay?"

"You have trouble with math?"

"A little." She sighed. "All right, a lot. If they hadn't invented machines to do arithmetic, I wouldn't be able to run my own business."

He gave her a sympathetic look. "That bad, huh?"

Riley nodded. "They have a fancy name for it now. A lot of people have this trouble," she added in her defense.

"You mean math anxiety."

"Uh-huh." She was embarrassed to admit such a thing to somebody with an obvious touch of mathematical genius. How could he possibly understand the terror that gripped her when she was faced with a column of numbers that marched straight at her, ready to do battle?

"The problem's curable, Riley."

"Sure is. And this is the medicine." She waved

her little calculator over the jumbled papers on her desk. "The great healing potion flows from two little double-A batteries, and I'll never be without them again. See?" She opened her desk drawer.

"My God, you must have twenty in there."

"Why not? They were on sale."

"But they might not all last until you need them."

Riley shrugged. "Some will, and like I said, they were on sale. The store took my credit card, so I stocked up."

"You used a credit card to buy batteries?"

"Of course. Then I have a record for the IRS. Batteries are a business expense." She didn't mention that she hadn't had enough cash at the time to cover the cost of twenty batteries.

Banning shook his head. "Don't be too loose with that card, Riley. I've seen several of my clients charge themselves into bankruptcy."

"Don't even say that word out loud," Riley said with a shudder. "It's bad luck."

"I don't mean to scare you. Just be careful. By the way, what's your plan for Shoe Mountain?" He bent his head toward the boxes stacked in front of her desk. "I don't see any appreciable shrinkage from last week."

Riley made a face. "And you know why? They're not Reeboks. Every executive I've tried to sell on that shoe insists on Reeboks. These are just as good, but they don't have the right name to be 'in.' It's so silly. I'd never carried sport shoes before, so I didn't realize people were so picky."

"And now you know," Banning said with a funny little smile.

She wrinkled her brow. "Uh-oh. What kind of sport shoes do you have? Or shall I guess?"

"They're good shoes, Riley."

"But so are mine!"

"I'm sure they are, but you've got to find a reason for people to buy them. How about cost?"

"Most of my customers don't care about that, but yes, they're cheaper. They're just the wrong brand."

"Then maybe you need a different brand of customer."

Riley regarded him thoughtfully. "Someone who needs a comfortable shoe but can't pay premium price."

"People who work on their feet all day."

"Banning! What if I took the Fancy Footwork van to an assembly plant?"

His eyes lit with approval. "You'd have to get permission," he cautioned.

"Yes, but if I got permission, and I went during lunch hour—what a brainstorm!"

"Your father would be proud of you," he said with a grin.

"Proud of us, you mean. You're the one who started me thinking about this." She beamed at him. "And I have a wonderful reward for you."

He looked into her green eyes and thought about the reward he would like to have—Riley in his arms, and not because they were sharing a motorcycle seat, either.

"You're coming home with me for a home-cooked steak dinner tonight. What do you think of that?"

"Terrific." He didn't give a damn about the steak dinner, but the going-home-with-her part suited him fine. Well, a home-cooked meal wouldn't be that hard to take, either. Trying to momentarily block out the heady appeal of her perfume, Banning tackled her paperwork with a vengeance.

When it was finished he suggested following her home in his car. He wouldn't be able to ride with her on the cycle, which was disappointing, but Banning gave that up willingly for a chance to be absolutely alone with Riley.

True, they were often alone together in the office, but the atmosphere didn't lend itself to romantic encounters. Besides, Banning had worked too hard creating a professional image to have it destroyed because a customer caught him in a clinch with his new office partner.

So he'd sublimated his physical attraction to Riley all week, although it was damn hard with that perfume hanging in the air and her habit of crossing her legs while she worked. He knew she hadn't planned it, but the angle of her desk gave him a perfect view of velvet thighs and shapely calves. It had been a long five days.

Her apartment house was on a hill, and she took him proudly out to the balcony and made him lean to the right until he saw a tiny slice of Puget Sound sparkling in the setting sun. A few sailboats were still out, dotting the water like scraps of paper.

"I had dreams of a bigger view," Riley confided, "but that will have to wait until Fancy Footwork is listed on the New York Stock Exchange, I guess."

"That's your goal? Shareholders and everything?"

"Sure, why not? Think big, I always say."

"I admire your ambition, Riley." He walked back through the arcaded doors to her living room. "And your furniture. Is this walnut?"

"Yes. You seem surprised."

"I may not know you as well as I thought. I expected modern stuff, lots of glass and chrome. This dark, carved wood is . . ."

"Old-fashioned?"

"Some people might say so. I like it." He looked around. "Makes this place warm and homey."

Riley accepted his compliment with a happy glow of satisfaction. "The store delivered it yesterday, just in time for your first visit."

"This is all new? We should be eating beans tonight, then. I wouldn't think you could afford steak after paying for this. It's got to be expensive."

"No problem. I bought it with delayed billing. I don't have to worry about paying for it until September."

His lifted eyebrow was indication enough of his opinion, now that she'd been around him for several weeks. Why had she blabbed that stupid bit of information? Maybe instead of Fancy Footwork her business should be called Fancy Foot-in-Mouth.

"But I'll have it paid off in no time, once I sell

those sport shoes as we've planned," she said quickly. "Would you like a drink? I have some bourbon, but that's all, I'm afraid."

"Thank God liquor stores don't take credit cards, or you'd probably have stocked a full bar by now."

"Banning, that's not fair."

He stepped toward her, his expression contrite. "No, it probably wasn't. I shouldn't have said that, but I worry about you, Riley."

"Afraid you won't get your rent on time?"

"*That* wasn't fair, either."

She sighed. "No, it wasn't. Let's forget about money for now, okay? Let's forget about the office, and business, and concentrate on a nice steak dinner." She clasped her hands in front of her and gave him an uncertain smile. "After all, you're my first guest. This is a special occasion."

He didn't know whether to shake her or cuddle her. And he didn't feel free to do either yet. "You're right. Can I still accept that bourbon?"

"You bet." She took a bottle from a nearby cabinet and headed for the kitchen.

"Can I help?"

"Absolutely not," she called, and reappeared in a few moments with his iced drink. "You did your part with my sales report. Now it's my turn to pamper you. Take off your jacket and tie and relax on my new sofa while I put the steaks in the broiler. I've got all the details covered."

He sat down on the plump cushions of her sofa, picked up his drink, and stretched one arm along the backrest. "How's that? Do I look comfortable enough?"

"You look great." The perfect decorator touch, she thought. No apartment should be without one.

"Care to join me?"

All at once she remembered her hostess duties. "I—I have a few things to do in the kitchen. Won't take long." She whirled and left the room, embarrassed by her gawking. Had he noticed that she looked at him the way a chocoholic might stare at devil's food cake?

Quickly she assembled her careful choices for dinner. At the restaurant last week Banning had mentioned how much he loved home-cooked food. Taking her cue, Riley had planned a meal that even she, a home-ec-class dropout, wouldn't ruin.

Steak was easy, just broil. And anyone could do salad—tear up a little lettuce, add bright cherry tomatoes and bell peppers for color, and voilà! French bread and a luscious-looking blueberry cheesecake came from the bakery down the street, a fancy little shop called Gourmet Quickies.

When the steak was in the broiler Riley took the bread from its wrapper and slid the cheesecake onto one of her own scalloped plates. Then she stuffed the bread wrapper and the cake box, both marked with the Gourmet Quickies logo, into the trash can. Why should Banning know all her secrets?

He didn't guess a thing. As they lingered over coffee and cheesecake, with the candle flames reflected in the polished walnut of her new and unpaid-for dining table, Riley congratulated herself.

"Fantastic meal," Banning said, taking his last bite of cheesecake. "If the shoe business doesn't pan out, maybe you should consider a catering service."

"I think I'll leave that sort of thing to Brit," Riley said. "I wouldn't want to plan meals for people on a regular basis."

"Not even every Friday night?"

She smiled at him. "That's different." But she wondered what she would do for an encore. Steak was her one and only company meal. Maybe Brit would send her a few foolproof recipes. "More coffee?"

"Let's take it over to the couch. I bet you haven't taken the time to enjoy your new furniture."

"That's true, I guess." Sit with Banning on the couch? How close? Was he thinking what she was thinking?

"Take your napkin," he instructed, picking up his cup and saucer. "We've got to protect this valuable stuff from scratches."

"I'm glad you're so careful. It's been a while since I've had good furniture, and I've forgotten how to treat it." Not since living with Jordan, she thought, and then the maid handled those worries.

Banning waited for her to sit down first, and she chose the exact middle of the sofa. After all, if she took one end and he the other, what fun would that be?

But when he sat down she wondered if she'd made a big mistake. His nearness, the faint smell of starch in his collar and after-shave on his chin, made her hand tremble as it held the coffee cup.

"I like this sofa," he said, leaning back and crossing one ankle over one knee. "Nice and deep. That's important if you're tall. I sit on some and feel like I'm in a pew at church, I have to stay so upright. And the edge of the thing catches me on the back of my thighs."

Riley gulped. She had a sudden mental picture of the backs of his thighs—naked. "I like to read," she said, setting her coffee on the table before she dropped it. "I saw this sofa and imagined burrowing in and escaping from the world."

"Sounds nice." He put his cup beside hers and stretched his arm along the back of the couch again. His sleeve brushed her hair.

She longed to lean back and rest her head against his arm, but they hadn't crossed that tiny barrier that would allow her to do such a thing. "Of course I won't be reading for a while yet. I have so much work to do with the business, and this apartment isn't finished by any means."

"Looks good to me."

From the sound of his voice she thought he might be looking directly at her when he said that, but she didn't turn her head to make sure. "But there's nothing on the walls! And I've taken all my plants to the office, so I have to buy new ones for here."

"You could bring a few back to the apartment. I wouldn't mind."

"Oh, no, I couldn't move the poor babies again. Spidey would give up if he had to make another transition. I'll just get more. And pictures, although I want something that will expand the space more than pictures. This room is small, don't you think?"

"Cozy."

"I've thought of mirrors, but I'm not sure. What this room really needs is a wall mural. They have some now that look as if you're standing at the top of a mountain, at the Grand Canyon, or at the edge of the sea. I wonder if—"

"Riley?"

"Yes?" She turned her head very slowly and found his lips only inches from hers.

"You're a terrific conversationalist."

She looked into the deep blue of his eyes and saw the same yearning that she'd glimpsed fleetingly several times during the past few weeks. "I am?"

"Too terrific." He reached up and ran the tips of his fingers along her jawline.

She imagined that her skin recorded his fingerprints, so completely did she feel his touch. And then his parted lips grazed hers. He pulled away, a question in his eyes.

She met his gaze, letting him see the excitement his whisper of a kiss had generated in her.

Once more his lips teased against hers, and at her muted sigh he slid his hand beneath her hair and took full possession of her mouth.

Riley had been curious about this kiss, wanted it to happen, but the force of her reaction took her by surprise. She began to tremble as desire rushed through her like a flash flood, sweeping every other thought away in a strong current of need. A little frightened, she pulled away.

"Riley?" He looked at her in confusion. "What is it?"

She struggled for breath. "I thought we could just kiss."

"That's all we were doing."

"I know, but I thought it would be just a kiss."

"It was."

"Not—not exactly. We . . . um . . . it's too soon for . . ."

"Didn't you like it?"

She looked away. "Maybe a little too much. I think—I think you'd better go home. For now."

He smiled. "For now?"

She stood up and took a deep breath. "Yes. For now."

He pushed himself out of the couch and picked up his sport coat. "You're sure?"

"Not very, but I wish you'd help me have a few scruples here, Banning."

"You have all kinds of scruples, and I don't see how my staying will endanger them."

"For me it will. You're my very first guest in my new apartment, and I just can't—"

"Okay," he said gently. "I understand. For now."

"See you on Monday."

"You bet. And we're still set up for Fridays?"

She found the courage to look into his eyes, knowing what he was asking. After their kiss, Fridays meant more than bookwork and dinner. "Yes, we are."

"Good." He brushed her lips once more and was gone.

She didn't move right away after the door closed behind him. She was afraid that if she did, she might run after him and call him back. But it was too soon for the emotions that clamored within her when they kissed. Perhaps her attraction was even dangerous, considering she and Banning were office partners.

No, she didn't really believe that. Banning wasn't her boss or anything. They shared an office, that was all. Why shouldn't they share a little more than that? But not quite yet. They needed to take it a bit slower.

The ringing of the telephone finally prompted her to leave the spot where Banning had last kissed her. Was he calling her so soon?

The voice on the line was male, but not Banning's. She thought she'd left that voice and the man it belonged to a continent away.

"Hello, Riley? I'll be in Seattle next Friday and Saturday. I have some business to discuss with you. How about dinner Friday night?"

CHAPTER FOUR

Riley's first thought was that she wouldn't tell Banning she had a date, no, *an appointment* with her ex-husband. On second thought, she knew she had to tell him. Above all, she wanted to be honest with Banning. She was upset that Jordan's appearance would interfere with their Friday-night plans and couldn't help wondering if Banning would miss their little time together too.

Yes, she'd be truthful with Banning, but she wouldn't tell him *everything*. She just couldn't.

Riley spent the weekend stewing about Jordan and why he was coming to see her. She thought she'd put a stop to his continued attentions by moving across the country. And now he claimed he had business on the West Coast. Next thing she knew, he'd announce he was moving operations to Seattle. What would she do then? Run from him again?

No. She was just getting settled here and she couldn't leave Banning without an office partner. He depended on her. And she on him. Plus, to be perfectly honest, she didn't want to leave Banning just yet. They'd shared only one kiss, but oh, what a kiss! With a sigh Riley knew she had to forget that for now.

As usual, Banning was in the office when she arrived Monday morning. Brushing one side of her dark mass of hair behind her ear, she approached his desk. "Banning, I'm glad you're here. I have something to tell you."

"Oh?" He raised his head curiously. "You haven't ordered more unsold shoes, have you? Or charged new office furniture?"

She glanced around at the oriental screen, then smiled at his teasing. "No. You know I wouldn't do that."

"Hope not." He shoved aside the file folders he had before him on the desk. "Okay, what's on your mind, Riley? Incidentally, dinner at your place was terrific. You're a fine cook. I hope you'll invite me over again."

"Why, thank you, Banning. Sure, I'll invite you over anytime. Except this Friday night. I can't stay after work and we can't—"

"Oh, you have plans Friday night?" He pursed his lips and nodded. "Okay."

"Well, they aren't plans that I wanted to have. I can't get out of them, although I'd like to."

He gazed at her benevolently. "Something's come up and you can't go out afterward. I understand, Riley."

"No, you don't! You see—"

"It's okay, Riley. You don't have to explain." His blue eyes softened. "It's no big deal."

"It isn't?" Her disappointment was keen that

they wouldn't be going out, but even keener that he didn't seem to care.

"I know your big concern is to get your sales totals done so they can be mailed Friday night. We'll just do them earlier in the day. And I'll take a rain check on dinner."

Her eyes lit up with a new thought. "What about Thursday night? I'm free then."

He shook his head. "I'm not." There was a moment of inquisitive silence and he explained. "I'm meeting a client who travels a lot. It's the only time he's free."

"Oh." She breathed a small sigh of relief. "If it's Gwyn, I understand."

"No, it isn't Gwyn. She and I"—he paused and shrugged—"aren't seeing eye to eye these days."

"Good. I mean . . ." Riley's quick gaze flew to meet his. "I mean, good, I hope this doesn't mess up your plans for the weekend."

"Only that we won't get to go someplace special."

"Maybe . . . maybe we could go on Saturday?" she proposed hopefully.

"Saturday?" Again he shook his head. "Sorry, I have a million things on Saturday."

"Oh." Her face fell and she tried to smile, tried not to show her deep disappointment. "Well, I guess we're left with Friday. That'll be fine. I appreciate you helping me with my darn books, Banning. More than you know. I just wish . . ."

"Wish what?"

"Oh, nothing." She turned slowly and walked back to her desk. She slumped down in the chair and chewed her lip. When she looked up Banning was watching her. She angled her head and asked, "Yes? What is it?"

"Uh, Riley, what if we worked on your books early Friday, then went down to the Pike Place Market for lunch? It's a neat place to shop and eat. Are you doing anything early Friday afternoon?"

"No, I'm not doing anything. Oh yes, Banning! That'd be great! I'd love it!" Happiness made her green eyes dance.

"It's an interesting area with some fascinating sights and sounds and people. I think you'll like it."

"I know I will. With you . . . uh, with you showing me around."

"Okay, it's settled then. We'll do your accounts early, then head out to the market."

"Thanks, Banning." Riley could hardly wait.

They worked on her books at noon, Banning intently studying the papers on her desk while Riley munched a handful of trail mix and checked on her plants.

"Hey, wouldn't you like to do some of this?"

"I was hoping you wouldn't ask."

"Come on, Riley. What happens if some Friday I'm not around?"

She walked over to him, her brow wrinkled in a frown. "You aren't planning to leave, are you, Banning?"

"No, of course not. I was here first, remember? It's my office. But what if I'd been out of town this week?"

She shrugged. "I'd be out on a limb."

His blue eyes narrowed accusingly. "And without a paycheck next week."

She nodded reluctantly and pulled a chair close to his side. "Okay, what do you want me to do?"

His finger scaled the first column of figures. "Here, total these."

Her gaze followed his hand and noted the scattering of curly hair on the top. It was a nice, strong, masculine hand. "Banning—"

"Do it, Riley, while I'm here to help you if you stumble. It does you no good if I always step in and rescue you. No one should be crippled by math anxiety. You need to learn how to handle this yourself."

"I feel like I'm back in school," she said with a groan.

"Um-hum, well, this is a test. Let's see what you've learned." His shoulder touched hers, emitting strength hidden beneath a button-down shirt.

She sighed and obeyed, punching the numbers into her own small calculator.

"And this one."

Again, she did as he instructed.

"Now, check the totals with these."

She poked the numbers he indicated and a slow grin began to spread over her face. "They're the same. I did it! I made them equal out!"

"Sure," he said proudly, touching her shoulder, letting his hand remain there for a moment. "See how easy? You can do it, Riley."

Her smile broadened. "Yeah, I can, can't I?"

"Absolutely." His eyes met hers and lingered just a little longer than necessary.

Riley smiled happily, delighted that she had added the column of figures correctly, especially with Banning watching her every move. When she hovered close to him like this it wasn't the math that gave her anxiety. It was Banning who set her heart to thumping and made her palms sweaty.

With her work done, all the columns totaled and corresponding, the sales report complete and stuffed into a large envelope, Riley turned on the answering machine and Banning locked the office door. This time it was Banning who suggested that they take the cycle.

Shoulders hugging. Large male hands lightly on her waist. Hips nestled tightly together. Thighs clutching. Banning and Riley swayed as one over each curve and hill. Clear ocean breezes whipped around them, the air off Puget Sound damp and salty and pungent. They parked the cycle, strapped the helmets to the seat, and started off down a narrow street.

She inhaled deeply. "I love the fresh air off the water!"

"Sometimes it's a little too fishy for me," he admitted.

"Don't you like fish?"

"Only to eat. Not to smell."

They laughed and he took her hand in a natural motion. "This is one of the oldest sections of town. Skid Row started here in Seattle," he informed her. "Back then it was Skid Road, a steep slope near the waterfront where logs were skidded to the waiting barges on the Sound. It was also an area where saloons and ladies of the night did a thriving business."

"Now that's a tidbit of information I couldn't do without," she said, laughing. "Have you ever thought of working for the Seattle Chamber of Commerce?"

"Too dull. I'd rather share an office with Riley Dugan. You never know what each day will bring!"

"Is that a compliment?"

"Of course it is," he said, slipping his arm casually around her shoulders. "You've added a much-needed element of excitement to my life."

"You have added lots to mine too," she said, smiling happily up at him.

The day was fresh and beautiful, the salty air invigorating, and they were together. Riley had never felt so comfortable and at ease as she did walking alongside Banning with her hand securely in his.

They entered Pike Place Market, an eighty-year-old farmers' market. It bustled with people selling everything from lettuce to oil paintings.

"A few years ago the city had plans to turn this whole space into a parking lot," he said as they dodged a kid hawking balloons in a narrow aisle.

"A parking lot?" She wrinkled her nose. "So what saved it?"

"The people. There was a great hue and cry. After all, this market is an institution in Seattle."

"You are a wealth of valuable information, Banning. I certainly chose the right tour guide today!"

"My pleasure," he said, steering her around three old fishermen arguing in the middle of the sidewalk.

She halted abruptly before a small, makeshift nursery filled with a huge array of green plants. "Oh, Banning, look! An azalea tree—and it's in full bloom. How beautiful. Wouldn't it look wonderful in my dining room, in that empty corner?"

"I guess so." Banning tried to look interested in the brilliant pink-blossomed tree.

Riley checked the price tag attached to one branch and whistled.

"Want to buy, miss?" A smiling oriental man approached her.

"How did you get it to bloom now? It's off-season, isn't it?"

"Special care."

"It's tempting," she said.

"Want to buy?"

"Do you take credit cards?"

"Riley . . ." Banning said.

"No cards, miss. Cash only."

Riley caught her lip between her teeth. "Thanks, but not today." She grabbed Banning's arm and started away.

He held back. "Look, Riley, if you really want it, I'll—"

"Heavens, no! Then you'd be feeding my bad habit."

"Yes, but you gave me these gray loafers, remember? And they're the most comfortable shoes I've ever owned. Let me do something for you."

"The shoes are a different matter. I wanted to

make up for not telling you I was a woman before I moved in. I didn't want us to . . ."

"Get off on the wrong foot?" he finished with a teasing wink.

"That's right, smarty." Laughing, she leaned her shoulder to his.

His blue eyes softened. "No chance of that now. We're in step together. And I want to get you that tree."

"No, I insist. I have to learn that I'm on a budget and can't afford everything I see. Anyway, how would we get it home on Cyclops?"

"You're right," he said, grinning. "That's practical logic. If it's the tree or me, I win."

"You sure do!" she said, and they continued down the sidewalk.

They ate fish fillets and bean soup and dark bread in a quaint little place overlooking the Sound. "You were right, Banning. I love it here. The food's great, and the sights are even better. All those bright sails look like colored confetti scattered over the water. What a lovely view."

"So are you when you smile like that. Are you happy here, Riley? Is Seattle everything you hoped for when you moved here?"

"It's much better," she said. "Better in every way. Except . . ." She paused.

"Except what?"

"Well, getting Fancy Footwork started has been slower than I expected. You saw what my sales looked like this week. Not great. But I did sell another pair of sport shoes."

."Only a hundred and eight to go," he said with a teasing grin.

"But I took your advice and made appointments next week with two industrial plants. Maybe they'll be interested in purchasing sport shoes if I take them to the plant. Wouldn't it be great? Why, if I could make just one big sale like that, it would solve all my problems. Most of them, anyway."

"A single woman like you shouldn't have any big problems, Riley. You're just getting your business started and you have to accept the fact that it takes time to make your profits count."

She nodded and fumbled with her tea glass. "I should tell you something, Banning. It . . . complicates my life somewhat. I'm divorced. Have been for about a year."

"That isn't a problem for me, Riley. Is it for you?"

"Well . . . in a way. Jordan's still trying to patch things up between us, even though we've been separated for a long time."

"Does he still love you?"

"He says he does. But I don't know. I only know he's very persistent. He . . . he's the one I have to see tonight."

"Oh?" Banning's eyebrows shot up. "Well, how do you feel about him?"

"Whatever we had is gone. Honestly."

"Then why are you meeting him?"

"I . . . we have some unfinished business. I just couldn't get out of it. He said he had some kind of deal going on here in Seattle, but I think he flew out here purposely to see me. He's done that sort of thing before."

Banning frowned and gazed out the window. "I see."

"No, you don't. It isn't the way it looks, Banning. In fact, I'm meeting him at the office so he won't find out where I live."

"The office? Then you want me out of there this evening."

"Not necessarily."

"Why, Riley, I wouldn't think of interfering in this little meeting. You certainly don't want me around when your ex-husband is there." There was an unmistakable acerbic tone to his voice.

Riley leaned forward earnestly. "But I'm trying to tell you, I don't particularly want to be alone with him. There's nothing between us anymore."

"Then why is he flying more than two thousand miles to see you? And why are you agreeing?"

"I told you, Banning, I can't get out of it. We have some unfinished business. But it's strictly business, believe me."

"I'd like to think that's true, Riley."

"It is, I swear it. I thought if I moved all the way across the country, Jordan would leave me alone. But he's at it again. I don't know what to do about him."

Banning looked intently at her. "What are you saying? That you want me to stay in the office? Or would you like for me to greet him and tell him you're too busy to see him?"

Her eyes grew large in alarm. "Oh, no, I don't want to make him mad. I . . . I'll handle him.

And I'll get rid of him. I . . . just . . . wanted you to know."

"Yeah, glad you told me. Now I know." Banning's jaw grew tight, and she could tell he was not pleased with the news.

Her hand slid tentatively over his before they left the restaurant. "Banning, have you ever been married?"

He hesitated only a moment before answering, "No. Never married. So I can't understand this hold he still has on you."

"Did you . . . really mean it when you said you hoped things between Jordan and me were strictly business?"

The tenseness in his jaws eased slightly. "Yes, Riley, I did."

"I'm glad you feel that way, because I do too." She dropped her eyes and dark lashes feathered her pink cheeks. Suddenly she was aware they were both revealing deeper feelings for each other than they had been willing to acknowledge in the past. "I think we'd better be getting back. Jordan will be there soon."

On the trip back to the office it seemed that when Banning sat behind her, he held her closer than before. But maybe it was just her imagination.

Banning staggered out of the car. It was already dark, but he recognized both Riley's van and her cycle in the office parking lot. He knew she wasn't home because he'd made a trip over there. Damn it, so she'd gone out with her ex, this Jordan guy,

after all. He should have known it wasn't as innocent and "completely over" as she had claimed.
And, like a fool, he had this damned tree to deal
with.

Banning grunted with the strain of his heavy
load and hurried into the revolving door. Getting
through was quite a feat. Where else could he store
it but in the office, along with a hundred and eight
pairs of shoes and several strange plants?

Originally, the azalea tree was meant as a gift for
Riley. Maybe now it was meaningless.

He shifted the heavy plant and punched the elevator button. Nothing happened. No lights, nothing. Then he remembered the elevator was always
switched off after eight o'clock.

Banning expelled a couple of expletives about
himself, the azalea tree, and two flights of stairs
before proceeding upward. What a fool he'd been
to feel sorry for Riley, to try and do something
nice for her when she was out somewhere having
fun with her ex-husband, a man with whom she'd
made love. Or maybe they were even making—oh
hell!

Gritting his teeth, Banning topped the second
flight of stairs. Hell yes, he was jealous. For only
one reason . . . he wanted Riley Dugan all to
himself.

Banning was puffing when he reached the office
door. Muttering more curses, he could see she'd
left the office light on. The least she could do was
consider the electric bill. He shifted the three-foot
plant, unlocked the door, and shoved it open. And
he stood there, staring through the lush green

leaves and profuse pink blossoms of the azalea tree in his arms.

"Banning!"

"Riley!"

"Who's this?" The unfamiliar voice belonged to a distinguished-looking man in a well-cut suit. His arms were folded across his chest and he leaned on Banning's desk. Obviously this was Jordan. Banning saw red—or was it brilliant pink from the blooming plant he was holding?

"Banning, what are you doing with that?" Riley stepped in front of the tree and bent one limb down to get a better look at him.

"Riley, what are you doing here at this hour? It's after dark!"

She wore a pained expression. "Talking to . . . uh, I want you to meet Jordan Ravenscroft. Jordan, this is my office partner, Banning Scott."

Jordan stepped forward with extended hand. Banning glared for a moment, biting his tongue to keep from saying something nasty about Jordan so casually lounging on his desk. Instead, he shuffled and staggered over to Riley's desk and plopped the azalea tree down beside it. Then he turned back to Riley and Jordan. The two men shook hands and sized each other up while Riley tried to make small talk.

"This is the same azalea tree we saw today, Banning. The beautiful one in bloom. What are you doing with it?"

Banning's mouth was tight and he felt the urge to knot his hands into fists. "I thought I'd surprise you, but looks like the surprise is on me."

"What? You mean . . ."

"Yeah. I'm a real sucker when you give me that sad little expression. I thought I'd cheer you up with this blooming freak you said you wanted."

"Banning, how sweet," she said softly, her green eyes switching from his face to the azalea.

Jordan moved to Riley's side and encircled her shoulders with his arm. "I know how you must feel, Banning. I've been trying to please this little lady for years. But now, looks like we're going to be partners again."

"What?" Banning immediately tried to disguise his shock. "That's just great."

"It's not true," Riley protested, wrenching out of Jordan's grasp. "Jordan, don't say that. We are *not* going to be partners again. Not if I can help it!"

"That depends on you, my dear," Jordan answered fluidly. "I would never force you into anything, but . . ." He shrugged and looked directly at Banning, commenting as if Riley weren't even there. "She was never very good at business practices, but she knows this is all in her best interest. When she has a little time to think about it, she'll realize it and come around."

"Damn it, Jordan, that's not true! Not exactly." Riley's voice grew shrill as she could see the situation being manipulated by her ex-husband.

"We might even be able to use a good CPA. Riley has always had trouble doing her books," Jordan said with a little chuckle.

"I'm not looking for any more clients," Banning lied, and stuffed his hands into his pockets. "Well, I certainly don't want to interfere in this little business you two have together."

"You're not interfering, Banning," Riley insisted.

"Maybe not, but I can see that I'm wasting my time. And yours." He strode toward the door.

"No, Banning, come back!"

But he was gone.

Riley glared at Jordan. "Damn you, Jordan. You must be quite pleased with yourself."

"Things will work out for the best, Riley. You'll see."

"Best for you, you mean!"

He shrugged. "For both of us, my darling."

"I'm not your darling!" She narrowed her green eyes. "Get out of here, Jordan. I don't want to see you again."

"But, my dear, you made a deal."

"I haven't forgotten the deal. I'll pay you back by Labor Day or . . ."

Jordan smiled. "Or we become partners again, my darling."

"You'll get your money."

"In a way, I have mixed feelings about this, Riley darling. If you don't pay up by September, I'll lose my investment in you. And if you open an office here for me, I'm sure it'll cost me additional money to help you run it. But it'll mean we'll be together more. And I'd like that."

"Well, I wouldn't. I know exactly how I feel about it, Jordan Ravenscroft. I intend to pay you off and never see you again." She turned her back on him and lovingly touched the azalea tree. "Now, get out of my office!"

The door slammed behind him, leaving her alone with her plants. And the new azalea tree from Banning. And a hundred and eight pairs of unsold shoes.

CHAPTER FIVE

Riley didn't consider herself a snoop, and going through Banning's desk on Saturday morning looking for his home address wasn't the most noble thing she'd ever done. But the situation called for desperate measures. She couldn't let the weekend go by without smoothing things over with her office partner.

At last she found something, a rental agreement for a motor home. He was due to pick it up the middle of August. Riley had trouble aligning her image of Banning Scott with motor-home vacation plans, but his name and address were on the reservation form. She had the information she needed.

After writing down the street and number, Riley returned Banning's papers to his desk and arranged everything exactly as she'd found it. Then she crossed to her own desk, spread out her map, and found the suburb of Bellevue, located on the east side of Lake Washington.

Crossing the Evergreen Point Bridge on Cyclops would be fun. She'd planned to take that ride someday, anyway. But confronting Banning wouldn't be much fun. Nevertheless, she had to do it and clear up any misconceptions Jordan had planted last night. Damn that man! Riley marveled that she once had been so impressionable and naive as to think Jordan Ravenscroft was wonderful.

On the way to Banning's house Riley contrasted Jordan's patronizing attitude as he claimed that she was "never very good at business practices" to Banning's calm insistence that she conquer her math anxiety. Jordan treated her like a little girl, always had. At one time she must have needed that, but now she found Jordan's behavior infuriating.

Obviously, so did Banning. Riley didn't care what Banning thought of Jordan, though. Banning's opinion of her was far more important. Yet she feared her confession this morning, no matter how necessary, wouldn't improve her standing with him.

She found his house, a freshly painted two-story, with no trouble. It seemed like a lot of room for one person. The gray sedan wasn't in sight, probably tucked away behind a closed garage door, but a Buick was parked in the drive.

Riley pulled her cycle to one side of the car. Did Banning have a visitor? She'd have to ask him for a few moments alone, regardless of who was here. Some things had to be said.

She rang the doorbell and tried to take deep, calming breaths while she waited. The time-worn technique didn't work. When Banning opened the door she felt as if a Saint Bernard was sitting on her chest. So this was what he looked like in jeans and a short-sleeved, casual shirt? And, of course,

his Reeboks. The transformation from businessman to casual bachelor created a powerful effect. If
he was appealing before . . .

"Riley? I'm surprised to see you here."

"We . . . we have to talk."

"Banning?" A woman's voice called from somewhere inside the house. "I'm not sure about this
bed."

"I'll be there in a second, Ann."

Whatever confidence Riley had left deserted her
as she stared up at Banning, horrified. "This is a
bad time," she muttered. "You did say you were
busy this morning, but I forgot. I'll—"

"Come in, Riley," he said abruptly, stepping
back from the door.

"I'll swing by later, okay? I want to tell you
something, but a couple of hours won't—"

"No. I'm damned curious about your reason for
being here. Come in and have a seat. I'll be right
with you."

Riley hesitated. Well, all right, what difference
did it make, whether she intruded on his privacy
now or later? He didn't look mussed, so evidently
he hadn't been involved in a passionate romp before he answered the door.

She'd say her piece and leave, simple as that.
Then he could get back to . . . whatever. Riley
tried not to think about the whatever, because, like
it or not, she was very unhappy that Banning was
involved with another woman. And not even
Gwyn!

Silently she walked into the living room and sat
on the edge of the plush sofa. "Nice room."

"Thanks. I'll be right back as soon as I settle her questions about the bedroom." Banning took the stairs to the second floor two at a time.

Riley wished he hadn't rushed up there so eagerly. While he was gone she glanced around at what looked like a professional decorating job in shades of blue. Not surprising on either account. Banning didn't seem much for interior decorating, and he wasn't exactly a bright-orange type of guy.

The morning paper was already tucked away in a brass magazine rack, along with a copy of *Business Week* and *U.S. News & World Report.* She saw no stray coffee cups or misplaced throw pillows.

In front of her a low oak table held an alabaster sculpture of a sea gull in flight. Riley ran a finger over the otherwise bare table. No dust.

At Banning's tread on the stairs, she glanced up.

"So," he said, choosing to remain standing with his arms crossed. "Did you and Jordan have a nice evening after I left? Reminisce about old times, maybe?"

He'd deliberately tried to put her on the defensive, but she was determined to keep her voice even. "Jordan gave you a false impression about our relationship, Banning. I don't want you to think that he and I . . ." She paused, unsure of how to complete the sentence, because she wasn't sure what Banning imagined, not really.

"I didn't want to draw conclusions, but the guy still has a hold over you. That was obvious, with all his talk about partnerships."

"We're not going to be partners!" She berated herself for allowing the pitch of her voice to rise.

"He's planning to open a branch of his import business in Seattle. He offered me the job of running it, but I refused."

"You did? Then I can't imagine what the two of you found to talk about for three hours before I arrived. Of course I'm assuming you talked. Maybe you found other things to do with your time."

That did it. All pretense of civilized behavior vanished as Riley leapt from the couch, shaking with indignation. "Like what? Is that your estimation of me, that I would conduct a lovers' rendezvous in our office? How dare you," she hissed. "I would never—" Riley stopped speaking as her gaze flicked to a tall blond woman descending the stairs.

"Banning?" the woman said hesitantly, coming into the room. "I'm trying to make do without you up there, but I need to know how you want the windows covered."

Riley's mouth dropped open. In all her life she'd never encountered a woman so brazen that she'd discuss the details of creating a bedroom hideaway in front of a complete stranger.

Banning turned. "Something to go with the rest of it, I guess. Lots of flounces. You decide. You have good taste. By the way, Ann, this is my new office partner, Riley Dugan. Riley, this is Ann Mathias."

"Pleased to meet you, Riley." The blond woman crossed the room and extended her hand.

In a state of shock, Riley took it. Polite introductions, yet? Banning Scott was far more complicated than she'd originally thought.

"Well, I'd better get back up there," Ann said with a smile. "Lots to do."

Riley's dazed mind couldn't comprehend what she meant. Lots to do in the bedroom? What was she preparing for Banning, some sort of orgy? And Riley had thought kissing Banning on her couch was heady stuff. He must have laughed all the way home at her lack of sophistication.

"Was that all you came for, to tell me you refused your husband's offer?" Banning prompted when Ann was gone.

"*Ex*-husband." She struggled to remember her rehearsed speech. Did it matter whether she delivered it? Yes, she might as well set the record straight, here and now. "First of all, I wanted to thank you for the plant. It's beautiful."

"Not one of my better ideas."

"Of course it was! And everything would have worked out perfectly except Jordan overstayed and you jumped to conclusions about what was happening."

"Riley, Jordan was still there because he felt a right to be. I could sense that the minute I walked in."

"All right, perhaps he does feel that way."

Banning's mouth compressed into a straight line. "If you refused his 'business offer,' why did he stay, Riley?" he asked at last, his voice deadly quiet.

"I resent your implication."

"I haven't enough facts to think otherwise. Why was he still there? If you really didn't want him to stay, you could have made him leave, unless you didn't want to."

"I wanted to, but I couldn't."

"Why?"

"Because . . ." She twisted her hands in front of her. "Because . . . I'm so afraid that telling you will make everything worse."

"Could everything possibly be worse?"

Riley thought of her fragile financial situation, of the scene last night in the office, and the woman waiting upstairs for Banning. "No."

"Then why don't you explain about Jordan? I have a right to know where I stand."

"Where you stand?" Riley began to sputter. "You have an incredible nerve, demanding to know where you stand, with a woman upstairs in your bedroom at this very moment," she continued, pointing at the ceiling, "preparing God knows what debauchery for the two of you when I finally leave."

"Debauchery?" Banning stared at her blankly.

"I may be slow, but I'm not totally stupid. First she consulted you about the bed, and then about covering the windows. And she has lots more to do, she said! I assume she's installing mirrors and assembling scented lotions!"

Banning's laugh began at the corners of his blue eyes, where the skin crinkled. Then his cheeks creased in a broad grin and he chuckled. The chuckle grew in volume until he threw back his head and laughed until the tears came.

Riley set her jaw. "I'm glad someone finds this amusing. I don't."

Banning wiped his eyes with the back of his hand. "You will someday," he said, gasping, "unless you have no sense of humor at all. That lady up there . . ." He stopped as laughter threatened to keep him from speaking. "Ann has been hired by me to . . . to redecorate my spare bedroom," he finished quickly as he cleared another chuckle from his throat.

Riley felt the heat of embarrassment climb up her neck. "An interior decorator?"

"Yep." Banning bit his lower lip to control a grin.

"You and she aren't . . . ?"

"Nope. I doubt if her husband would be overjoyed by that prospect. Or her two children. Ann and Bill are clients of mine, and when I bought this house, she did the living room. I wanted it to look nice."

Riley felt her face grow hotter. "It does."

"And you're blushing." He closed the gap between them and tipped up her chin with one finger. "Embarrassed?"

She avoided his gaze. "Unbelievably. My goodness, what you must think of me, with my talk of mirrors and lotions, and—"

"Sounds interesting." His lips hovered closer to hers. "Maybe we should discuss what you know about such things. I'm pretty ignorant, myself."

She looked into his blue eyes at last and saw the passion reflected there. "I'll bet."

"Honest." His other hand touched her waist, guiding her gently into his arms as his lips sought hers.

The remembered pressure of his lips swept away the agony of her embarrassment and replaced it with slow-burning desire. He drew her against his chest, and with a sigh she leaned into his embrace, experiencing for the first time the hard planes of his body pressed against her. Instinctively she reached up, circling his neck with her arms to bring him even closer.

She felt the rapid vibration of his heartbeat and knew it was matched by hers as his tongue explored the moist recesses of her mouth. She met his foray with light teasing of her own, and a muffled groan emerged from his throat.

Gasping, he pulled away. "Time out." He turned away and rubbed the back of his neck. "Whew! I don't think you know the meaning of 'just a kiss,' as you phrased it last week."

"Don't blame me! You started—"

"Hold it. Okay, I did. And I probably shouldn't have. After all, you haven't really explained anything yet."

Riley tried to pull herself together. "No, but I will. The truth about Jordan is that—"

"Banning?"

He spun toward the stairs. "Yes, Ann?"

"Sorry to bother you again, but are we keeping the built-in shelves or getting new—"

"Take it all out," Banning said with a wave of his hand. "Everything goes. Gut the place. I don't want it looking like an office anymore." He brought his attention back to Riley.

"Fine." Ann blinked and looked more carefully at the two people in the living room. Crossing to the briefcase she'd left in the hall, she cleared her throat. "I'll be going now, Banning. I'll call you next week about fabric samples and furniture styles."

"Okay." He half turned. "Thanks, Ann."

"Sure." With a tiny smile, she closed the door behind her.

Banning sighed. "As you were saying?"

"I started Fancy Footwork when I was still married to Jordan."

"He implied as much last night, in that damned superior manner of his. What's the problem, did he give you the idea or something? Is that why you feel obligated?"

"No. It was my idea. And . . ." Riley forced herself to say it. "And his money."

"His money," Banning repeated. He studied her face. "That's an elaborate van."

Riley nodded.

"You don't own it."

"No. Not much of it, anyway. I've been trying to pay him back, but with the move, and now office expenses, I can't seem to come out ahead."

Banning muttered an earthy curse. "And he's just the kind of jerk who'll use that debt to manipulate you into doing what he wants. You've got to pay him back, Riley."

"I know." She opened her mouth to tell him about the September deadline, but decided against it. She'd probably been foolish to set that deadline, but at the time it seemed the only way to get rid of Jordan. Her ex-husband didn't expect her to pay him back by September, so he'd been willing to leave, thinking he had his victory. But she would pay him back. Somehow.

"We'll figure out something," Banning said.

"Did—did you say 'we'?"

He smiled at her. "Aren't we office partners?"

Her heart gave a little leap. "I thought for sure when you found out about all my debts you'd want to throw me out."

He looked at her for a long time. "You are in a precarious financial spot."

"I'm afraid so."

"And you've taken on the additional burden of that furniture."

She lifted her chin. "But I don't have to start paying until September. By then I'll be able to handle it."

Banning shook his head and sighed. "You're also an incurable optimist. But I admire your spunk, even as I cringe at your fiscal problems."

Riley knew, despite any negative comments Banning made, that she now had an ally. She looked at him standing there, so much more approachable today in his casual clothes, and she began to tingle with longing. Did she have more than an ally? "How do you spell that? The kind of problems I have?" She took an imperceptible step toward him.

Banning caught the challenge in her green eyes. Tucking his hands in the back pockets of his jeans, he surveyed her from head to toe. Her black stirrup pants covered the legs he'd grown to love looking at. A black oversized blouse with jagged swatches of color all over it pretty much camouflaged the rest of her. And for the first time he could remember, she wore no earrings.

"That's *fiscal*, with an *f*, although in that outfit I can't tell much about you *physically*, with a *ph*. I'll have to rely on memory."

"Do you have a good memory?" She stepped nearer.

"Like an elephant, especially when it comes to certain things."

"Such as?" She was close enough to reach out and touch him, but she didn't.

"Such as the way you sit in your desk chair, with one leg crossed over the other, and your skirt inching up. Once I almost swallowed a paper clip."

Riley smiled. "Fortunately I can perform the Heimlich maneuver, if that should ever happen."

"If I'd known you were so talented, I'd have faked something."

"Really?" She ran the tip of her tongue over her upper lip.

Banning took an unsteady breath. "I think you know what you're doing, you little tease."

"Then or now?"

"Both." With an athletic quickness he grabbed her and pulled her roughly into his arms. "You're driving me crazy, Riley Dugan." He bent his head and placed tiny kisses along the side of her neck. "And you know it," he murmured against her skin.

"Why, Banning," she said breathlessly, tilting her head to better enjoy the tingle of his lips on her throat, "whatever are you doing?"

"If you don't know, I must be doing it wrong."

"Oh, no," she murmured, as his kisses crept upward to the corner of her mouth and sure hands moved her hips into sync with his. "I don't think you're doing anything wrong."

His touch was magic, and when he led her up the stairs she went willingly, longing to quell the ache that had been building inside her since the first time she saw Banning Scott.

Fleetingly, she noticed that his bedroom was austere in much the same way his office had been before she initiated some changes.

But there was nothing austere about the way he made love. His kisses were rich confections, beginning with light sweetness and building to an intense sensuality that left her feeling drugged.

After kicking off their shoes they tumbled upon the neatly made bed fully dressed, and at first neither made a move to reduce the barrier of clothes between them. Face to face, they explored the delight of lips, teeth, noses, cheeks, eyebrows, and, of course, ears.

Boldly, Riley ran her tongue around the inner curve of his ear and felt him shudder. "I hope you're not ticklish," she murmured, and he shuddered again. "Because you have such inviting ears."

"I'm not ticklish," he said raggedly. "That's very nice. Very . . . nice."

"Good." Riley breathed warm kisses along his jawline and lay back on the pillow, assessing the results of her attentions.

Smoky blue eyes looked directly into hers as his

hand eased from the small of her back and slipped under the smooth fabric of her blouse. His fingers brushed her skin in slow circles. Gradually he increased the pressure of his caress.

When he spoke his voice was husky. "I have to know if I should . . . if you're . . ."

"Yes," she said, understanding his question. "I've taken care of that . . ."

Her answer unleashed the last hint of restraint in his touch. Massaging her spine, he edged toward the clasp of her bra. He held her gaze as he unfastened the catch and traced the faint indentation of the elastic around her rib cage to the satin underside of her breast.

She lay perfectly still as he stroked upward with his knuckles until he reached the puckered nipple. He circled the aureole with the tip of one finger and she moaned softly.

"You're trembling."

"I can't help it."

"Neither can I."

She laid a hand against his chest and felt the fine tremors going through his body. Slowly she unfastened the first button of his shirt.

He mirrored her action, his fingers working their way down the front of her blouse.

When she reached the waistband of his jeans she stopped. Sliding her hand inside his shirt, she pressed her palm against the taut muscles of his stomach.

He finished his unbuttoning and started to push the blouse aside, but his fist clenched around a handful of the material as she rotated her hand over his skin, working upward to the nipples hidden in swirls of chest hair.

"Oh, Riley," he said, expelling a held breath and closing his eyes for the first time. "God, I want you." When he opened them again his eyes were ablaze with passion, and the hands that whisked her blouse and lacy bra from her shoulders were not quite as gentle as before.

She whispered his name as he bent his head to the swell of her breast. When he slipped his hand beneath the elastic waistband of her slacks, she arched her hips, allowing him to pull the garment from her desire-wracked body. The time for slow exploration was gone. She wanted him deep inside her.

For an agonizing moment he was gone while he finished removing his clothes. Riley watched the lean perfection of his body emerge and pressed her thighs together as the throbbing within became almost unbearable at the sight of him.

He returned and gathered her close, winding both arms and legs tight around her for a searing kiss that imprinted on her body a forever memory of rippled muscles, the sweet abrasion of hair-roughened skin, and the smooth shaft that pressed a furrow in the softness of her belly. She writhed impatiently in his arms and showed him with undulating hips what she wanted.

With a groan he rolled her to her back and lifted his body a few inches away from hers. "You're incredible," he gasped. "I've never—"

"Banning." Boldly she reached for him, stroking him intimately.

"God." He thrust forward with age-old instinct into her moist softness and moaned with pleasure as she rose to meet him. He felt the intensity of newness and yet, unexplainably, the warmth of recognition.

He sensed her rhythm and joined it, but the rhythm was his as well. He could read her body in ways that had been closed to him with other women. Or maybe it was her doing, her openness that showed him how to please. So easy. So right. The fullness built in him, and he knew her tension matched his.

Her motion changed, and a roaring echoed in his ears, like surf, as he forgot everything but the overwhelming urge to push into her, again and again. His control was gone. Nothing mattered but the bursting need within him. At the final moment he heard two voices crying out. One must have been his.

As sanity slowly returned he found that he'd buried his face against the side of her neck. Glossy dark hair tickled his nose, and her scent made him want her again, despite the fact that he should be completely sated.

"What . . ." He swallowed and tried once more. His voice sounded strange. "What was that perfume again?"

Her lashes fluttered open and she turned her head to smile at him. Her eyes were very green. "Obsession."

CHAPTER SIX

Banning watched her sleep. It had been a long time since he'd watched a woman sleeping with such feelings of warmth and affection. And it had been many years since he'd had such a pleasant day as he had yesterday with Riley. And oh what a night! He'd almost forgotten what it was like to have genuine fun with a woman, and that was a sad commentary on how his life had turned out. And how it had evolved from the old life he'd once led in Hawaii.

But from the very first day Riley Dugan walked through his office door, his life had changed. Routine nine-to-five working days were no longer routine. She added a spark to everything she did. And a smile to everyone she touched. Especially him. Oh God, he needed this woman—needed her laughter, her teasing fun, her loving.

Unashamed, he recalled how they had loved last night. Riley was an eager, creative lover, never failing to excite him or holding back her own affections.

They spent the afternoon hiking through Washington Park and the Arboretum. Riley had ended up being the one to give him the tour, spouting full explanations of all the strange plants. And he had loved every minute. Last night, instead of going out, they had rented a movie for the VCR and sent out for pizza.

Then they made love. He hadn't felt so contented and sexually satisfied in . . . years. Twelve years, in fact.

Riley sighed in her sleep and snuggled against his bare chest. She was beautiful with her smooth, creamy skin next to his rough, hairy body. Her dark sweep of hair fanned over the pillow, tousled and sexy. Black, feathery eyelashes, resting against pink skin stretched over high cheekbones, hid her gorgeous green eyes. Her lips were slightly swollen from a night of kissing, the lower lip sensuously pouting. Those sweet lips had sent him to heaven during the last twelve hours more than once.

She shifted and her beautiful eyelashes fluttered open. She smiled shyly at him and stretched like a young kitten, first one arm, then the other. "Morning. Have you been awake long?"

"Long enough to decide you're beautiful." He traced her nose and the curve of her lips. "And I'm a lucky man to have you in my bed."

"I'm a mess now. No makeup and my hair all over the place."

"I like you like this." His palm caressed her cheek, then tenderly stroked her disheveled hair.

"Have you been lying there just watching me?"

"Hmm," he acknowledged, trailing his fingertips along her neck and down to one uncovered breast. His thumb rubbed over the perky nipple, making it harder. "And thinking."

"Thinking about what?"

"About you and me. How well we go together. And how much I've missed by not having you around sooner."

"That would have been hard to do, seeing as how I just arrived in Seattle a few weeks ago."

"I wish we'd known each other earlier in our lives, Riley."

"I thought I'd made it into your bed pretty quickly, myself. Maybe too quickly."

"Never." He moved to kiss her pouting lips, then dipped down to taste that puckered rosebud tip on her exposed breast.

"Banning, this won't ruin our office partnership, will it?"

He gazed at her for a moment, then laughed rakishly. "Ruin what? No, Riley, nothing could ruin that. Change it, maybe."

"Change it? How?"

"Like this." He lowered the covers to expose both of her creamy breasts and alternated kissing each one until the peaks rose sharply to greet his lips. "I don't know if I can stay away from you. Can't keep my hands off you now that I've touched you everywhere."

"Oh, Banning . . ." She drew him closer. "You had me worried for a minute. I thought you were going to say we couldn't be office partners and lovers too."

"If I had to make a choice, I can tell you which I'd pick." He nuzzled her neck. "Actually, it might make things at the office even more lively and interesting than they have been in the past. I told you my life was extremely dull before you showed up. And now—"

"Now it's chaos," she said, giggling as he began to kiss a particularly ticklish spot on her belly.

"Now you keep me up day and night." His lips moved over her caressingly, ending up close to hers. "And I can't imagine being without you, Riley."

"Then you've forgiven me for meeting with Jordan in our office?"

"Forgiven you a thousand times," he muttered between kisses. "What we have to work on is that debt to him."

"We? You mean—"

"Riley." His face moved close to hers. "Hush. It's time for us, not the world."

She touched the broad chest hovering over hers and let her hands explore the muscles of his shoulders. Spreading her palms flat on his back, she pulled him down to her. A thrill shot through her as she felt the growing strength of his maleness against her thigh.

"Oh, Banning, what you do to me . . ."

"Good. Because you do the same to me." His lips captured hers in a sweet kiss that grew in depth and intensity—touching, tasting, exploring until they both were breathless. "Only more. Just looking at you takes my breath away. And I want you again."

"Love me . . ." she begged in a whisper.

And while the morning fog shrouded the neat,

two-story house, Banning and Riley made love in the upstairs bedroom. By the time they lay still and sated in each other's arms, the morning sun had evaporated most of the fog and was beginning to brighten the day.

"Riley, I'm exhausted."

"I'm hungry. What's for breakfast?"

His only response was a low groan.

"Well, I can fix something. What have you got?"

"Leftover pizza."

"Ugh!" She wriggled to free herself from his embrace. "I'll check. But first, a shower."

A few minutes later she emerged from the bathroom wrapped in towels from head to toe. "Uh, Banning, I hate to be a bother, but do you have a bathrobe or something comfy I can put on?"

He rolled over and examined the towel-draped figure before him. "No bother. In the closet. Take anything you want."

She did.

When she emerged wearing a shirt he didn't recognize, Banning sat up in bed. "Where'd you get that?"

"In the back," she said, smiling and pirouetting in a red plaid shirt that came to mid-thigh and looked like it belonged on a logger.

He smiled with masculine pleasure and applauded her cheerfully. "Looks better on you than it ever did on me. Now I remember. Dear old Aunt Mavis from Peoria sent it to me for Christmas several years ago."

"I'll bet you never wore it."

"Nope. It just didn't seem to be my style."

"Well, it's just right for me," Riley crowed. "It feels wonderfully soft and warm."

"You can have it, then, if you'll let me feel."

"I'd rather leave it here, for those spontaneous times I might need it."

He grinned. "Is that a promise? There'll be more spontaneous weekends like this one?"

"Depends," she said mysteriously. "On what I find in the fridge to eat. A girl can't be expected to go hungry, now can she?"

"Absolutely not! You go ahead and see what you can find. I'll grab a quick shower and join you in a few minutes."

She started to go, then stopped. "Oh, uh, Banning, you wouldn't happen to have a nice little bakery down the street, would you? Or a deli, open on Sundays?" She was thinking of the convenient Gourmet Quickies near her own apartment house.

"Nope. You have to do it yourself in this neighborhood."

"Why are you stuck way out here, anyway? There aren't any conveniences nearby. And this house is too big for one person."

"I like lots of room."

"Not me. I don't want to clean any more house than I just have to," Riley admitted. "But my friend, Brit, formed a business in Washington for people like me."

"Is she successful?"

"Very. She has even incorporated robots into it. She and her husband program the robot for your particular household. I have high hopes of getting one of those robots someday."

"Is that before or after September?"

"After!" she said with a laugh, and skipped downstairs to the kitchen. What in the ever-loving world could she easily prepare for breakfast? Maybe now her secret would be revealed—she couldn't cook worth beans.

Riley scouted the refrigerator and pantry and found them fairly empty. Typical of a bachelor's kitchen. Just a few cans, a couple of eggs, some basic spices, and flour. Briefly she considered calling Brit long-distance but decided against it. There were certain situations an independent woman handled by herself. Maybe Banning had a cookbook.

She found several old cookbooks in a bottom drawer, obviously not used very much. One in particular caught her eye and she grabbed it up desperately. *Hawaiian Love Bites.* Curious, she opened and read a neatly penned greeting on the flyleaf: "With love to my own Cutie Buns!"

Cutie Buns! Riley laughed out loud. Obviously this was something from Banning's past. Hastily she thumbed the yellowed pages and an old snapshot fell out of the book's center and dropped onto the floor. "Must be Cutie Buns," she muttered, reaching to pick it up.

Her smile faded slowly as she examined the photo. A much younger Banning clad in a brief swimsuit and boasting almost shoulder-length hair smiled jauntily at the camera. One hand braced an upright surfboard and the other draped around a beautiful blond, clad in a tiny bikini. The girl was perched on the seat of a shiny, black Harley-Davidson motorcycle. The carefree happiness apparent on their faces made it obvious that they were lovers.

Riley tried to shrug it off, but a strange feeling came over her, overwhelming her for a few miserable moments. The photo blurred and her hand shook. Just seeing Banning in earlier years, so obviously happy with another woman, sent her ego spinning. Jealousy, that's what it is, she admonished herself. And it's ridiculous to be jealous of something that happened years ago.

This was now and Banning was hers. She gasped and clapped her hand to her lips. Was he? Is that what she wanted? At that moment she realized that, indeed, she wanted him to be completely and totally hers. Her heart was captured by the present Banning, the one she knew, not the one in this old photo.

Riley tossed the aged photo down on the table and grabbed the cookbook, thumbing through it quickly. She had something to do, had to work on what was happening today. She spotted a starred recipe, and instantly deduced it was a favorite. That was the one she'd fix. Scanning the ingredients, she concluded that any simpleton could make it.

The surprise was in the oven and the last can opened when Banning strolled into the kitchen. He was neatly dressed in a casual open-necked shirt and Levi's and smelled fresh and wonderful. His hair was slightly damp and falling across his forehead. This man was a far cry from the one in the photo. Riley couldn't imagine him wheeling across a sandy beach with a blond girlfriend cling-ing to his back and a surfboard under his arm. She shook her head to clear the vision. It was all wrong.

"Hi. You hungry yet?"

He picked the photo up off the counter. "Where'd you get this?"

She shrugged and said lightly, "It fell out of this cookbook, the one to Cutie Buns."

"Cutie Buns? Where'd you hear that?" His voice was strangely demanding.

"I read it in the cookbook."

"Oh." He looked back down at the photo.

"I barely recognized you in that picture, Ban-ning." Riley dumped the last can of fruit into the bowl of ambrosia she was concocting. "Is she an old girlfriend?"

"Yeah, well, it's . . ." He paused and turned away. "It's an old picture."

"I can tell that by your hair." She brought the bowl of fruit to the table. "I didn't know you were a surfer."

"In my former life, I was a beach bum."

"You were? That's amazing! I can't imagine." She sat down and curiously watched his rather sharp reaction to the photo. He held it gingerly and walked to the window and stared.

"Where were you? California?"

"No, in"—he paused to clear his throat—"in Hawaii."

"Hawaii? Boy, when you go, you really do it up right!"

His expression grew tight and distant. "You said it there. Do I ever."

"Well, I think it sounds exotic, living in Hawaii, surfing every day. Just what thousands of kids would love to do."

"Oh yeah?" he muttered sarcastically. "It was a wise move, all right, quitting college and moving to Waikiki all in one week."

"You make it sound like a criminal offense, Banning. Actually, sometimes a little fling is good for the soul. Sowing the wild oats, that sort of thing."

He glared at her. "My little fling, as you call it, managed to mess up not just my own life but several others. Now, how good is that for the soul?"

"Well, I don't know. How much did you mess up your life? You seem to be doing all right now."

"It's taken me years to catch up. I told you I quit school, for no more reason than I was bored and tired of cold weather. Gave up a full scholarship to Loyola and went to live on the beach."

"Of course you would look at it differently now that you're older and more mature. But it sounds like something a kid from Illinois might do."

"Ha!" he grunted. "I wasted four years of my life, working odd jobs and riding the waves. When I finally came to my senses and decided to go back to school, I had to work full-time and borrow money too. It took me five years to pay back that damned loan. I still haven't recovered from the financial setbacks."

"I can see how your fling made it harder on yourself," Riley conceded.

"Harder on everyone."

Riley nodded to the photo in his hand. "On her? What did you do, love her and leave her?"

Banning's jaw twitched as he worked to control raging emotions. Finally, in a strained tone, he responded. "I loved her and left her pregnant."

A long agonizing moment of silence followed.

Riley finally found her voice. "I can't believe it, Banning."

"Well, believe it. That's what I did. Now do you see me differently, Riley? Your dull, conservative office partner has a rather checkered past."

"We all have things in our past that—"

"That we regret the rest of our lives?"

Her lips tightened and she nodded. "Sometimes."

He ran a hand through his rumpled hair. "I was such a fool."

Riley lifted her chin and looked at him steadily. "The man I loved last night and this morning is not a fool. He's smart and gentle and understanding. The man I share an office with is tolerant and generous. I don't even know the man who went to Hawaii and lived on the beach."

"And didn't have enough money or maturity to be responsible for his own life, much less others."

She trembled beneath his oversized red shirt. "No one is perfect, Banning. From my experience, mistakes are pretty normal."

"Not this one."

"What happened, Banning? Tell me."

His eyes implored hers, searching for truth and reason. "Do you . . . do you really want to hear this, Riley?"

"Yes." Her voice gentled. "I really do." She took his hands and led him to the table. They sat down opposite one another, and when Riley saw the awful pain on his face, she wanted to make all his hurt go away. And yet she knew instinctively that it was not in her power. This was something he had to overcome. But she could show him she cared. And that his past, no matter how checkered, didn't matter to her.

Riley also knew, without another doubt, that she loved Banning with all her heart. "Tell me about it," she encouraged softly.

He took a deep breath. "Kim and I were in love. I thought we were, anyway. We had a carefree lifestyle on the beach, partying constantly, working whenever we needed a few bucks. The pregnancy threw me for a loop—it was so unexpected. In the beginning she told me she was on the pill and I didn't think any more about it. Then she started having side effects from the pills and we switched to other methods, figuring they were just as good."

Riley nodded. "But they weren't."

"When she announced that she was pregnant I wanted to do the honorable thing and marry her. Hell, we loved each other, didn't we?"

"She didn't want marriage?"

"To a beach bum like me? Hell, no! You see, she came from a wealthy family in Hawaii and they had better plans for her than the likes of me. I had nothing to offer her or a child. *Our child.* And they were right. I was penniless. So, she took her folks' advice and dumped me and went back to Big Daddy."

"Did she . . . did she have the baby?"

Banning's face changed. "Yes. I have a daughter, Riley. She's twelve years old and I've never seen her."

"Never? Why? Oh my God, Banning, how awful. Never seen her?"

"Kim's family kept us apart, and when the baby was born they got a court order preventing me from coming around. I had no money, no job, no power. It became too much of a hassle and so I finally left Hawaii."

She reached for one of his hands. "How awful, Banning. To have a child and never get to see her."

"Oh, as Zabrina got older and began to ask questions about her real father, Kim admitted I was alive on the mainland and we started a sort of correspondence. I have pictures of Zabrina. Want to see?"

"Yes, oh yes!"

He reached for an album on a small corner bookshelf and opened to a well-worn page. There was a succession of school photos, showing the growing-up progression of a beautiful brown-haired child. She went from scraggly curls to pigtails to a chin-length bob.

"Banning, she's beautiful."

"I think so too." He chuckled, but Riley could see the pride in his eyes. "Course, I'm prejudiced."

"You have a lot to be proud of. She's going to be a lovely young lady."

"Yeah . . ." He lifted his head and sniffed. "Riley, what do I smell?"

"Smell?" She hopped up and screeched. "Oh dear! The popovers! They're ruined! Damn it!"

She pulled the smoking pan from the oven. Banning joined her and they gaped at the dark brown wads in the muffin tin. "Oh, no! I baked them specially for you! I wanted to do something for you, something you liked. . . ." She looked up at him helplessly. "I forgot about them while we were talking. I'm sorry, Banning."

He looked at her gently and put his hands on her arms, drawing her closer. "Riley, I can't believe you're so upset over some dumb food."

"But I wanted to fix something you really liked. And I knew you liked these popovers because they were starred and—"

"Riley, Riley, you're wonderful." He kissed her nose affectionately. "Even after hearing all this about my past, you still want to please me? I thought you might be upset, even angry."

"None of that matters to me," she murmured softly. She framed his face with her slender hands and reached up to kiss him. Her lips met his with gentle persuasion at first, and when he could no longer resist the insistent pressure, he succumbed.

His arms wrapped around her back and he hauled her firmly against his lean body and kissed her long and hard. When they finally broke apart he murmured, "I was afraid you'd want to end this before it went any further when you heard how irresponsible I was."

"You certainly aren't irresponsible now, Banning. Anyway, it wasn't all your fault."

"Yes, but I was the one with no job prospects, no

future. If I'd been in better financial shape, Kim's parents wouldn't have taken the stand they did. And I would never have had to miss knowing my daughter."

Riley couldn't help thinking, *And I'd never have had the chance to know you*, but she didn't reveal her torn feelings. "You mustn't ever forget about her, but don't take all the responsibility. Kim was half of that team effort, and the last I heard, that's how babies are made."

He smiled in spite of his emotional strain. "I think it still works that way. Riley, you're amazing."

"Because I figured out how babies are made?"

"No, because you have the amazing ability to put everything in its proper perspective. *Yours.*"

"Am I wrong?"

"No, my darling Riley. You know just how to make me feel okay. Better than that, you make me feel wonderful."

"That's the best compliment I've heard in a long time," she said, smiling up into his eyes. "You didn't even say that this morning."

"You didn't give me a chance. When you hopped out of bed, I was still weak and breathless."

"Weak?" she said, gripping one bicep and squeezing. "This is hardly weak."

"You're a very special lady, Riley. And I'm a damn lucky man."

"And I'm still hungry. How about some ambrosia, food of the gods? I found a few cans of fruit and I know it's not as good as fresh, but it'll have to do. And now, with no popovers—"

"It's okay about the popovers. We all make mistakes."

"And don't you forget it," she said earnestly.

They ate the ambrosia quietly, each lost in thought. Finally Banning laid his fork down. "Riley, I haven't told you everything. But knowing how you feel about me having a daughter, you'll probably be glad."

"What? Zabrina has a twin?"

He took her hand and cradled it between his. "Zabrina is coming to visit me this summer. That's why I'm redecorating the spare bedroom. It's why I have this big house out in the suburbs. I want to look respectable in my daughter's eyes. In three weeks I'll meet Zabrina for the first time in my life. And she'll meet her father. While I'm anxious for it to happen, the idea scares the hell out of me."

Riley took a quick breath and stared at him. Her first thought was how this unknown daughter's visit would affect her newly developing relationship with Banning. And, at the moment, she didn't want anything or anyone interfering, not even this love child who meant so much to him.

CHAPTER SEVEN

Monday afternoon Riley pulled the red van into the Emerson Title and Trust parking lot. As she walked toward the building her shadow stretched ahead of her and rippled up the concrete steps. It had been a long day, and she was tired, but a good kind of tired. Shoe Mountain had been conquered.

She delighted in her achievement of this one small victory before Banning left on his business trip the next day. Her success would help convince him that she was resourceful and competent instead of a financial liability.

He'd be surprised. Early this morning, as he'd helped her load one hundred and eight shoe boxes into the van, he'd warned her not to expect to sell the whole bunch on the first try. But she had done exactly that, except for one pair, which she now tucked under her arm. She could have sold it, too, but she wanted to present Banning with an official souvenir of Shoe Mountain.

Once in the office, she was disappointed to discover a client sitting in front of Banning's desk. Keeping her expression neutral, she gave him a little wave when he lifted an eyebrow in her direction. This particular news was for Banning alone, their own private triumph, and she wasn't about to blurt it out in front of a stranger.

"I'll be able to help you unload in a few minutes, Riley," Banning said, returning to the client's paperwork in front of him.

"Fine." She sat in her desk chair and swiveled toward the wall so that he wouldn't see her grin. What a day! She switched on her hot plate and brewed herself a cup of tea.

While sipping on the hot liquid she listened to the messages on her answering machine. She might as well return a few calls while Banning finished with his client. She picked up the tail of her Garfield telephone and watched the sleeping cat's eyes open. The sight never failed to amuse her. Work could be fun if a person worked at it.

She might never enjoy the Friday-night sales reports, but thanks to Banning's tutoring, she handled the paperwork almost all by herself. Once in a while she asked him to check her math, but he seldom found mistakes anymore. Jordan would have been amazed.

Riley punched out the number of her first phone call and leaned back in her chair. Glancing sideways at Banning, she deliberately crossed her legs at the knee. He caught her movement and casually began to chew on the end of a paper clip. It had become their silent joke when someone was in the office and they both wished the person would leave.

At last the man shook Banning's hand and departed.

Banning crossed his arms and leaned forward on his desk. "Hi, gorgeous."

"Hi, yourself."

"Time to reassemble Shoe Mountain?"

Riley could barely curb her excitement. "You never did believe I could do it, did you?"

"I'm from Missouri, the 'Show Me' state."

Riley laughed. "You're not. You're from Illinois."

"That's close enough. God, I want to hold you, Riley Dugan. Why isn't it five o'clock yet? I've got someone else coming in any minute." He stood up. "Let's unload your van. Maybe I can steal a kiss in there."

"Sounds nice, but I've already unloaded the van." She picked up the single shoe box and walked over to his desk. "And this is all there was to unload. Here. They're not Reeboks, but you can wear them in the house where nobody can see."

He stared at her incredulously. "One pair is all you have left? Did you dump them in the Sound?"

"I sold them!" She couldn't contain her pride any longer and threw her arms in the air. "Every damn pair, and I could have sold these, too, but I saved out one box in your size for old time's sake."

"How is that possible?"

"One woman knew all her kids' sizes and bought shoes for all of them. Several people took more than one pair, for when the first pair wears out."

"At your suggestion, I bet."

"Yep."

"What a saleswoman!" He charged around the desk and swung her up in his arms. "That van

119

must have been rocking and rolling with all the people in and out of there."

"It was crazy," she admitted, winding her arms around his neck and laughing up at him. "If you hadn't been drilling me on math, I would have freaked out. But I handled it, and I've got a hunk of cash to put toward my debt with Jordan."

"Fantastic." He gazed down at her, blue eyes smoky with desire. "And you're fantastic. How am I going to make it without you for the next few days? If the account weren't so big, I'd cancel this trip to Spokane. Come with me, Riley."

She shook her head. "You'll only be gone until Thursday, and somebody's got to mind the store, Banning. That's one of the benefits of having an office partner, remember?"

"That's not the benefit I'm remembering right now," he said, rubbing suggestively against her. "Oh, damn, I hear footsteps in the hall. Must be my four-thirty, right on time, doggone her."

"Why, Banning, I thought you admired punctuality."

"Not at this very moment." Reluctantly he released her and straightened his tie. "Later, sweet lady." He gave her a smoldering look and returned to his desk. "And thanks for the shoes. I think I'll wear them tonight while I chase you around the house. Why, come in, Mrs. Mansfield! Nice to see you again. How are those grandchildren of yours?"

Riley smiled at the gray-haired woman and retreated to her desk. Tonight she would stay at Banning's house and see him off in the morning. In the past two weeks she and Banning had enjoyed each other without restraint once the business day was through. Whether they were at his house or her apartment, they made love spontaneously, and not always in the bedroom, either.

But after this Sunday she could hardly expect the same easygoing relationship with Banning, considering that his twelve-year-old daughter would be living with him for two weeks. For part of that time Banning and Zabrina wouldn't even be around. He'd asked Riley to cover for him while he took his daughter to Disneyland. That's what the motor-home rental had been all about.

At no time had he mentioned plans to include the three of them. Would he want Riley to become friends with Zabrina? If so, he hadn't set up any opportunities for that to happen, and Riley was too proud to bring the matter to his attention.

"Ready to go, super-saleslady?"

Banning's question brought her out of her deep concentration and she realized Mrs. Mansfield had left and Banning was straightening up his papers.

"You bet." She brushed aside her uncertainties about Zabrina and vowed to make the most of the time she had alone with Banning. "Tonight we'll celebrate conquering the slopes of Shoe Mountain."

"The landscape has definitely changed."

"Don't you think the area looks bare? Maybe I need a few more plants to—"

"Riley."

"What?"

"Methuselah and Spidey have enough playmates. Mrs. Mansfield asked if I'd started a sideline business in potted plants."

"Now there's an idea! We could—"

"No."

"Spoilsport."

He stood up. "If you'll come home with me, I might be able to change your mind about that evaluation."

"Oh?" She took pleasurable inventory of the lithe physique that made his dark blue suit fit so well. "Sounds interesting."

"With you, Riley, it always is." He met her gaze with a look of undisguised passion. "Let's go."

She stacked her files and pushed away from her desk. "You've convinced me."

"Good. Besides, I want you to see Zabrina's room. It's almost done."

"Okay." *Zabrina.* The girl's name kept popping into the conversation, whether Riley liked it or not. "I'm sure it looks great."

"I hope she thinks so."

"She will."

On the drive to Banning's house Riley made idle conversation, but her thoughts kept returning to Zabrina and what the girl's reaction would be to all her father's preparations. Suppose Zabrina loved her room, loved Seattle? Suppose she'd had enough of Hawaii and wanted to live with her father permanently? Kim's parents could hardly object to Banning's life-style now.

There. Riley had admitted her greatest fear, that Zabrina would become a permanent fixture in Banning's life. If Banning had a daughter to worry about, how could his relationship with Riley continue in the same uncomplicated way?

Riley thought about her friend Brit, who had fallen in love with a man who had children. In that instance the children fell in love with Brit, right on cue. But Riley had seen enough of life to know the opposite could happen. She and Zabrina might not even like each other.

Several times in the past two weeks Riley had almost spoken her love to him, but something held her back. Perhaps it was Zabrina's impending visit and Banning's omission of any plans that included Riley. Damn, but the timing was so awkward.

"I guess selling all those shoes wore you out. You haven't said a word since we crossed the bridge."

Riley snapped her attention back to the present. "Sorry," she apologized with a smile. "I guess I was wondering how to spend all that money."

"Riley, it's spent."

She chuckled. "I know. Just trying to get a rise out of you."

"Oh, lady, you never have trouble doing that."

"Banning Scott, such talk," she teased.

"I know, and I'm through with talking. I want action."

"A man of action. I like that."

An hour later she thought of how much she liked his particular kind of action. They'd left a trail of clothes from the bottom of the stairs up to his bedroom before throwing themselves with abandon into a joyous romp that left them both sweat-slicked and glowing with fulfillment.

"Come on," Banning said, leaping up and rummaging through his closet for the red shirt that had become her favorite outfit after they made love. "I'll show you Zabrina's room. And I have a favor to ask."

"You picked the right time. I'm bursting with gratitude right now."

"Me too. Any favors I can do for you?"

"I'll let you know later." She winked as she put on the red shirt and he pulled on a navy robe.

They padded barefoot to Zabrina's room and stood side by side in the doorway with their arms wound around each other.

"Whatcha think?"

"It's very . . . elaborate."

"Ann describes it as every little girl's dream."

"I'm sure that's true, Banning. The room looks sort of like the inside of a cotton-candy machine."

"That's because it contrasts so sharply with everything else in the house. I guess I like things plain and simple."

"So I've noticed."

"But Zabrina's a young girl. I didn't want her to feel strange here."

"You keep saying how young she is. From what you told me, she should be about twelve by now."

"That's young."

"When's her birthday?"

"September the third. God, it's hard for me to believe I'll be the father of a teenager."

"Banning, do you have any sisters?"

"Nope. Just a brother. Why?"

"I wondered if you'd been around twelve- and

thirteen-year-old girls much. They can be very—
uh—changeable."

Banning looked uncomfortable. "You mean their
approaching womanhood and all that stuff? I'm
sure Kim has told her all about that."

"I'm sure she has, and I didn't really mean you'd
have to give a lecture on the birds and bees." Riley
touched his cheek. He was in for quite an experience, meeting his daughter for the first time at this
volatile time in her life. "I was remembering how
their tastes can change dramatically. One minute
they like lace and pink ruffles, and the next purple
and orange stripes."

"Well, yeah, when they get into high school and
everything. Zabrina's only going into eighth
grade."

Riley wondered if he clung so stubbornly to the
belief that Zabrina was still young because he'd
missed knowing her as a little girl. But eighth
grade wasn't the world of childhood anymore.
Zabrina probably had a boyfriend and a collection
of rock albums. Riley couldn't picture an almost-
teenager sprawled across the frothy pink bed-
spread with its matching canopy over her head.

"What was that favor you mentioned?" she
asked.

"Oh. The wallpaper." He gave her a quick
squeeze and walked over to the white French Provincial dresser. "I've got a sample in here." He
opened a drawer and took out a square of white
paper with tiny pink rosebuds on it.

"I'm not a whiz at putting up wallpaper, Banning."

He laughed. "That's not the favor. Ann's hired someone to do it, but the stuff isn't coming in until after I leave tomorrow. Would you supervise, make sure everything's okay? It shouldn't take long, and you can turn on both answering machines at the office for a couple of hours."

"I'd be glad to help." Riley felt a warm glow of hope. Maybe she did figure into Banning's life. He could have asked Ann to take care of the wallpaper business, but he'd chosen her to make sure his daughter's room turned out the way he wanted it.

"Great." He replaced the wallpaper sample in the drawer and crossed the room. "I'll give you a key to the house," he added, taking her in his arms. "I should have done that by now, anyway."

"Oh?" Riley felt like dancing. That had to mean she was more than a casual fling.

He gazed affectionately into her eyes. "Most definitely. And as long as you'll have a key, why don't you plan to be here when I get home Thursday night? We'll have some catching up to do."

Riley kissed the firm ridge of his jaw. "Sounds nice."

"And don't dress up." Banning slid both hands beneath the hem of the red shirt. "This is my favorite outfit."

"Lady, this is what they gave me. I don't know nothing about no little pink rosebuds."

Riley stared at the rolls of wallpaper lying on the floor of Zabrina's room. It was pink and flowered, as Banning had ordered, but the resemblance stopped there.

126

"Don't start anything until I've made a phone call," she instructed the wallpaper hanger.

"You're the boss."

Riley fished in her purse and found Ann Mathias's business card. Then she picked up the gilt-edged receiver of Zabrina's French Provincial telephone and dialed the number, taking care not to break a nail in the process.

"Concepts Interior Decorating."

Riley recognized the voice of the blond woman she'd met several weeks ago. "Ann? This is Riley Dugan. Did you change the wallpaper order for Zabrina's room?"

"No." The woman sounded puzzled. "Why?"

"Have you seen what came in?"

"I didn't bother to look this time, because Banning said you'd be there this morning. Maybe I should have."

"I think so, Ann. The flowers are huge pink things with enormous green leaves. It looks like the attack of the giant peonies. Zabrina will have nightmares with this on the walls."

"Sounds awful. Damn that company. And we don't have time to reorder, either. That's the second time they've screwed me up like this. I'm definitely switching suppliers."

"Do you have anything else in stock that's close?"

Ann sighed. "Not really. I guess I'll leave the walls white and look for some framed prints. Maybe a couple of soft watercolors."

"Ann, did Banning ever mention to you how old his daughter is?"

127

"He didn't say exactly. Just told me he wanted something very frilly and feminine that would make a little girl happy."

"She's almost thirteen."

There was silence on the other end of the line. "Let's hope she's immature for thirteen," Ann said at last.

"Let's hope."

"I wish Banning had told me her age, but he was so adamant about the decor, and in my business you follow directions or lose clients."

"I understand. Besides, nothing can be done about it now. Zabrina will be here on Sunday. And the room is beautiful, Ann. Maybe she'll love it."

"Maybe. Now I'm not sure what to get for the walls, though."

Riley thought quickly. She'd noticed the special two-for-one sale this morning in the paper and dismissed it because she had no use for two. And yet it might be the perfect solution, set before her by the hand of fate. What was one more credit-card bill, considering her debt-ridden situation?

"I have an idea, Ann. I'll handle the wall decoration."

"I hate to dump this in your lap, Riley."

"You're not. I'm offering. This will give me a chance to do something special for Banning and Zabrina. I'd like that."

"Well . . . okay. I'm sure he'll be delighted with whatever you do. Let me know how it turns out."

"Sure will." Riley hung up the phone with a sense of excitement. This project would be just what she needed to keep her from missing Banning so much during the next two days.

She sent the wallpaper hanger away and hopped on Cyclops. A two-for-one sale didn't come along every day, and she could end up with something for herself as well as a solution for Zabrina's blank bedroom wall.

Riley made her purchase and spent the afternoon clearing up details at the office. By six that evening she had changed to old clothes and was back in Zabrina's room spreading a pasty substance on the wall. The store clerk had called it "sizing."

"Okay," she mumbled to herself. "I have to let it sit for a while. How long did they say? Oh, well. Awhile. Let's see how this will look." She began unrolling sections of a tropical beach scene on the carpet.

Perhaps the palm trees and sunlit sand didn't quite mesh with a canopy bed and French Provincial furniture, but Riley figured it would remind Zabrina of home. And the colors certainly jazzed up a room that was so nauseatingly sweet it almost gave Riley a sugar high.

Figuring the sizing wasn't ready yet, Riley padded barefoot downstairs to brew herself a cup of tea. She drank slowly, but when the tea was gone she could wait no longer. She had to see some results.

She mixed the glue quickly and spread it on the first section of the mural. After pressing it in place she moved to the second section with growing excitement. This would be such fun! Brit had never agreed to having one in their shared apartment, and with Jordan a wall mural had been out of the question.

By the time she was gluing the third strip, the first was curling from the top. Riley smashed it back into place. By the fifth strip, the first one had fallen completely from the wall and the second and third were threatening to follow.

"Damn it! What's wrong?" Riley fumed, rushing from strip to strip pressing as hard as she could. Frantically, she kept working. Once the whole wall was up she'd be able to handle any little trouble spots.

The trouble spots grew. As fast as she pounded one strip back in place, two more curled downward and rustled to the floor. Riley grabbed Zabrina's phone with pasty fingers and called the store where she had bought the mural. She broke two fingernails in the process.

"What's wrong with my stupid mural?" she practically shouted into the phone. "It won't stay up!"

"Did you leave the sizing on for an hour and a half?" the clerk asked politely.

"Pretty close," Riley fibbed. Half an hour was more like it. That should have been plenty of time. Wasn't this the modern age?

"And the glue had to sit for a minute and a half before you used it."

"It did?"

"I told you about that."

"I forgot. And the last strips are staying up a little better. In fact, the very last one is—oh, no,

130

'there it goes! I have to hang up." Riley slammed down the receiver and rushed to rescue the one section that had seemed permanent and was now curling away from the wall.

"I can't stand it," Riley wailed. "This has to work. It just has to. Damn it, stay up there!" She pounded the mural with her fist. "Be strong! Be sticky!" But the minute she let go, the paper rolled to the floor.

Finally she backed away from the wall and stood in the center of the room looking at the curling sections of her beautiful mural. What could she do?

Then, with a snap of her fingers, she bounded down the stairs and out to the garage. Soon she was back.

"You're going to get yours, you stupid mural. Right in the coconuts." Holding the top corner of the scene in place, she found a dark section of palm fronds and swiftly hammered a nail into the paper. "*Now* see if you can fall off, you stickless wonder."

She worked quickly, finding strategic spots where the nailheads wouldn't show unless someone scrutinized the scene. Within a half hour Zabrina's room had a breathtaking view of a remote Hawaiian beach and Riley rode home, too exhausted to tackle the mural she'd chosen for herself.

Wednesday and Thursday dragged as Riley waited impatiently for Banning to come back from Spokane. She splurged at the Gourmet Quickies shop for a special meal to welcome him home.

With a twinge of guilt she shredded the boxes

and stuffed them to the bottom of his garbage can. Soon she'd have to admit that she couldn't cook, but not tonight. Not with only three days remaining before Zabrina came to town. Riley remembered the anxiety she felt years ago when she was about to meet Jordan's mother for the first time. Her nervousness about Zabrina was similar, but in a strange way it was worse. Was it because this time her heart was really on the line?

"Riley?"

Joy flooded through her at the sound of his voice, and she ran into the hallway. "You're home!"

He dropped his briefcase and closed the space between them. "God, I've missed you," he murmured, gathering her against him for a deep kiss.

She breathed in his scent appreciatively and pressed her body against his gray linen suit. Had it been only two days since she'd felt those strong arms around her? It seemed forever. Gratefully she absorbed the solid feel of him.

At last he lifted his lips from hers, and his breathing was labored. "I love that smell."

"Lamb stew?"

He shook his head. "That perfume you wear. My nose had dreams about it the past two nights. Did I mention how much I've missed you?"

"You can mention it again."

"I've missed you like I wouldn't have believed possible, Riley." His blue eyes were serious. "Thank you for being here."

"I've missed you too. A lot."

"I hoped you would. You look luscious as always in my red shirt."

Riley giggled.

He reached underneath it to cup her behind. "And nothing else," he said with a ragged sigh as he drew her against him. "This is some welcome, Riley. How about continuing it upstairs?"

She snuggled against him. "I might be persuaded."

"Then let's go." He wrapped his arm around her shoulders and guided her toward the stairs. "While I can still walk."

"Gladly."

At the top of the stairs he glanced in Zabrina's room as they passed the open door. Then he came to an abrupt halt. "What's that?"

"A surprise." She gave him a smug smile.

He dropped his arm from her shoulders and strode into the room. "I didn't order a wall mural."

"There was a big mistake. We had to do something. The rosebud wallpaper order got messed up. The design the company sent had huge pink flowers and big green leaves. It was ugly, Banning."

"So whose idea was this?" He walked over to the wall and looked at the scene from ceiling to floor and side to side. Almost tentatively he reached out and touched the wave, letting one finger trail along the white crest.

"Mine," she said proudly. It *was* an impressive wall and she loved it. This was one of her better brainstorms. "The mural brings a little piece of Hawaii to her room, don't you think?"

He turned slowly and gazed at her for a long time, a strained expression on his face. "Riley, this just won't do."

CHAPTER EIGHT

Icy apprehension gripped her. It had never occurred to Riley that Banning might not like the mural. "Why not? What's wrong with a beach scene?"

"Anybody can see it doesn't go with the rest of the room."

"That's because it isn't cotton candy and marshmallows."

"What's that supposed to mean? The other wallpaper was pink flowers and things."

"What it means is that your daughter may be beyond the pink-flower stage. I think she'll like this, Banning. At any rate, she can have both. The frilly canopy bed on one side and a beach mural on the other."

"How do you know what she'll like?"

"I don't, exactly. Of course she's an individual with her own individual taste. But she's almost a teenager and most would love something like—"

"Zabrina's only twelve. She's just a child! Don't go pushing her beyond her years. That's what's wrong with kids today. They aren't allowed to be kids."

135

"Well, you're certainly allowing that."

"And I intend to continue."

"Interesting statement from a man who's never seen his daughter. Listen, Banning, girls of this age are so sensitive and changeable. They're on the verge of being women, yet in some ways are childlike."

He folded his arms across his chest. "Is this going to be a lesson on child development from someone who has no children?"

"I can remember being thirteen not too many years ago. It can be a tough age."

"Why do you keep saying she's thirteen? She's only twelve!"

"Because she probably thinks of herself as thirteen if her birthday is only a month away. Twelve is an in-between age, but thirteen is advanced."

"*You* may have been advanced for your age, but my daughter isn't."

"I have three sisters and they all couldn't wait until they were teens. Do you think my whole family was advanced?"

"Maybe," he said stubbornly. "The fact that you have sisters makes you an expert on young girls, I suppose!"

"No, but it does give me an edge."

"Not when it comes to picking wallpaper. I'm sorry, Riley, but this one has to go. And the sooner we rip it off, the sooner Ann can put something else up here." He turned around and reached for the corner.

"Rip it off?" Riley flung her back against the wall. "No, Banning! You can't do that!"

"Why not? It has to go, Riley."

"It can't go!"

"Riley, please get out of my way—"

"It won't go."

He loomed closer.

Instantly a protective instinct emerged and she spread her arms out, encompassing the clean, sunlit sand on one side and the swaying palms on the other. Beyond her fingertips a cerulean wave curled white scalloped edges and appeared ready to crash onto the immaculate beach. She couldn't let him destroy it, not after all her hard work.

"Banning, look up. At the coconuts."

He took a closer step and his gaze focused upward, then swept around, halting at the various, shiny-dotted additions to the mural. "What the . . . ?" He scratched his head and went back to the coconuts, which seemed to glare back at him with shiny silver eyes.

"Riley, what is this? What the hell . . . ?" Even as he said it he didn't want to hear her answer. He was afraid he knew.

"Nails," she mumbled feebly.

"Nails?" he yelled. "Nails all over the wall? Nail *holes* in my wall?" He seemed to be having trouble getting enough air. "W-why?"

"Now, take it easy, Banning. Let me try to explain. I got this easy-to-install mural kit and I thought it would be easy. But it wasn't. Now, I know how you feel about nail holes, but these were necessary."

"Necessary? You mean, nails came with the kit?"

"No, er . . . well, maybe not absolutely neces-

137

sary, but at the time . . . you see, what happened was . . ."

"I'm trying to be patient, Riley." He folded his arms across his chest.

She went on rapidly. "Once I got started, I discovered the darn glue wouldn't hold the paper up. I had strips of the mural everywhere, some rolling off the wall. Some had already fallen off and rolled up on the floor."

"Sounds like a damned mess to me."

"Well, it was near, I guess. Plus, it was getting late and I couldn't go buy more glue. I kept working on it, doing my best. I held it up on the walls until my arms ached. But it still kept falling down. I had no other alternative."

"You couldn't wait until the next day when you could get some help?" His voice held an incredulous tone.

She shook her head. "No, I couldn't. I had to finish it. Don't you understand? Once I started, I *had* to see it completed." She could tell by his expression, he couldn't understand. "Oh, Banning, if you don't look too closely, I'm sure it'll be okay."

"I can't believe it. You fixed this damned thing so I can't even take it off the wall. Certainly not before Zabrina gets here. How could you do such a"—he paused to take another breath—"such a—thing. What do you expect me to tell her? Don't look too closely at the mural because you might see the nails?"

"I have a feeling she won't care nearly as much about the nails as you do, Banning. Why don't you let Zabrina decide how she likes the mural? If she

138

hates it, I'll be glad to pay for having it completely redone."

"*You'll* pay? On your budget? Ha! That's a laugh!"

"Damn it, I will, Banning! I'll hire somebody who knows all about walls and can fix those nail holes so nobody will ever, ever see the repairs. And then I'll have it covered with the tiniest, pinkest little rosebuds you ever saw! And you'll be happy as hell!"

With that she stormed out of the room, put her clothes back on, and left him alone to stare at the Hawaiian beach scene on the wall in Zabrina's room.

Riley rode Cyclops home from Banning's like a bat out of hell. She didn't know when she'd ever been so mad. Or so disappointed. What did he know about the aesthetic value of wall murals, anyway? What did he know about teenaged girls? And what did he know about her? Obviously nothing.

It infuriated her to think he could be so narrow-minded and stubborn. Well, she could be stubborn too. That damned mural had taken her the better part of one evening and he could care less about her efforts and time. Not to mention her feelings.

He should be glad she didn't put the beach scene on the office wall. She came darned close.

As she mulled over the situation Riley realized that Zabrina might very well take one look at the mural and dislike it. But that was her privilege, as the one who'd be occupying the room.

By the time Riley was parking Cyclops in her space at the apartment house she had decided she could handle the situation if Zabrina wanted the mural changed. She wouldn't mind discussing other possibilities with Zabrina and helping her pick something else out. In fact, it might be fun.

But Banning had taken all the fun out of the whole episode. He seemed hung up on the idea that Zabrina was a child. Of course she wasn't a woman, but Riley would almost bet she wasn't the kid Banning thought she was. What was wrong with him, anyway? Why did he want to perpetuate her childhood?

Riley stormed into her apartment and halted to admire her own mural, the other half of the two-for-one deal. Just as she'd hoped, it made her living room look immense and she loved the feeling it gave.

Her mural was quite different from Zabrina's, though. It was a field, just a lovely, stretching-out-forever field of tall grasses, like much of the heartland. On a distant hill two young girls strolled, hand in hand, picking wild flowers.

It reminded Riley of home and the closeness she shared with her friend Brit. They'd been best buddies growing up, and Riley missed her now—missed those wonderful, youthful days when they'd been so free and innocent.

Riley stayed home that night, alone and lonely. And she wondered what Banning was doing, if he was sulking or if he was busy scraping the beach scene off his daughter's wall.

* * *

The next day she was busy with client appointments until afternoon. When she finally made it back to the office, Banning was gone. In a way she was relieved. It avoided the inevitable confrontation. In another way it merely prolonged it. To keep from thinking about him and their spat, she kept busy with her routine, end-of-the-week paperwork.

About four in the afternoon he appeared. He gave her a contrite look and walked over to her desk. "Riley, I'm glad you're here. I, uh, had to meet a client and it took longer than I expected."

She remained cool. "Yes?"

"Well, I'm back now and can help you with your sales reports."

"Thanks, Banning, but I just finished them."

"You did?"

"You sound disappointed. This is what you've been trying to teach me, isn't it? After all, I never know when you'll be out of town."

"Yes. Of course, yes. I'm . . . I'm glad you managed without me. Did everything add up?"

"Sure." She stood and gave him a forced smile. "Well, I have an after-five appointment with a client. Guess I'd better be going." She reached for the doorknob.

"Uh, Riley, wait a minute."

She turned around, a question on her oval face.

"I, uh, oh hell. I'm sorry about what I said last night. It's—the mural's not so bad, after all. And I had no right to make you feel so bad. I know you were only trying to help."

141

"Thanks, Banning. I'm glad you realize that. Well, see you."

She waited for his response.

"See you." His jaw tightened as he watched her leave the office. Well, hell, he'd apologized. What more did she want from him? Obviously she'd been hurt, and he'd been an ass last night. But he had acknowledged that.

Damn it, he didn't want her going home alone. Or worse, searching out someone else to keep her company. And he didn't want to go home without her, either. But what could he do?

Banning stared around the office, his gaze lingering on the items that spoke so distinctly of Riley. And enhanced the spirit of the office. Most of the spirited stuff was hers. His spirited stuff was packed away in the box in the storeroom, awaiting someone to dump it. But he hadn't discarded it. Maybe because he just couldn't bring himself to throw away all those memories.

Then he snapped his fingers. He knew what he'd do to get her attention, if he still remembered after all these years.

Riley slipped into her apartment after dark. It had been a long day, a miserable week. But her sales quota had more than doubled. She should be happy, but she wasn't. The time without Banning, then their argument, had drained her and she felt empty without him.

Another lonely night without Banning. Oh, he'd apologized, but so what? Words were only . . . words. He was obviously preoccupied with the arrival of his daughter in two days. And she had botched his little girl's perfect room.

As she walked through the living room Riley paused to admire her mural. Affectionately she touched the two children playing on the hill. Then she headed upstairs to her bedroom. She'd take a shower, crawl into bed, and read a book. She was turning down the bed covers when she first heard it. And she thought a neighbor had turned a radio extra loud. But no, it wasn't very modern music. It was somewhat jazzy, sounded like . . . a ukulele.

Ukulele?

She ran back downstairs to her balcony and leaned over the rail. There, standing in the rhododendron plants, was Banning strumming his old ukulele and singing his heart out. When he saw her he increased his volume and sang to the tune of "Has Anybody Seen My Gal?":

> Riley, please, on my knees,
> With my best apologies,
> Will Riley Dugan be my gal?
> Oh those eyes, oh those lips,
> Oh those sexy, swinging hips,
> Will Riley Dugan be my gal?

Riley laughed and applauded. How could she resist him? He was marvelous! God, how she loved him.

Immediately Banning launched into another verse:

My life was tame, before you came,
With kisses divine,
Hold me tight, every night,
Love your body next to mine!

Could she woo, could she coo,
Could she, could she—

"Banning, please stop!"

"You like my singing that much, huh?"

"You're crazy! What are you doing down there?"

"Trying to get your attention."

"Well, you did. And all my neighbors too."

"Want to hear the next verse?"

"No! Not from there." She leaned over the rail and grinned. "Come on up."

"Thought I'd have to sing out here all night before you invited me in." He climbed out of the garden below her balcony and went around to the front.

She swung the door open. "You didn't have to go to such extremes."

"I wanted you to know the depth of my sincerity."

"Tell me." She stepped back and he joined her inside.

"I've missed you like hell this week."

"Me too."

They stood silently facing each other. The look was magic. They drew together with a sudden frantic fierceness, as if time and emotions had deprived them of the sustenance for life. Had deprived them of each other.

"Oh God, Riley, I didn't mean to hurt you."

"Banning, I never wanted to make you mad."

Then they were in each other's arms, pressing fervent kisses to lips and cheeks and necks. Their fully clothed bodies writhed together, erotically enhancing their enflamed passions.

His mouth seized her sweet lips, molding to their shape, captivating her with his wild craving. His tongue played along their sensitive outer edges, tasting and touching with fire. Slowly, daringly, he penetrated her mouth with his tongue, seeking her life-giving, spirited flavor, wanting her with an overwhelming rush.

She responded heatedly to his entreaties, opening for his invasion, seeking his fulfilling gratification. She'd dreamed of his kiss this week, awakened in a cold sweat thinking he might never return to her, that she might never feel him naked and needing her again. She clung to him, trapped by her growing desire.

His tongue circled her lips, then pushed deeper into her mouth, sending her soaring with uncontrolled yearning. She surged against him, lost to this sensation of their merging. She longed for more and thought she'd die if he stopped now.

But Banning had no intentions of stopping. His hands stroked her back, sliding over the silky material of her blouse, finally pulling it from the confines of her skirt and slipping his hands underneath to touch her heated skin.

"Oh, Banning . . ." she breathed low. "I thought you'd never come back to me."

"Riley, I couldn't stand it without you. I want

you so." He unbuttoned her blouse and stripped it off her shoulders. The bra was next and he cradled her breasts for sweet, sensuous kisses, lifting them to his lips and continuing to stroke and admire and murmur words of love.

She removed his shirt and kissed the broad expanse of his chest, pausing to lave his taut nipples with her tongue. With a low groan he pulled her close, crushing her breasts to the muscular wall of his chest. His kiss left her breathless.

Then his hands unzipped her skirt and scooted beneath her panty hose. As his hands guided the hose off he stroked the entire length of her legs, touching her thighs, knees, calves, all the way down to her feet. She shivered as he caressed each foot and bent to kiss the arch and inside the ankle. All the while his hands never stopped stroking her.

When he stood again she reached for his zipper. "Now, Banning."

"Here?"

"The sofa. We'll christen it tonight." She was delirious with desire and spoke freely of her love as he lowered her to the flowered cushions. His knee pressed between her legs, and with a soft sound she relaxed and waited for him. His moist kisses tantalized her whole body until she was aflame, gyrating against him, impatient for his hard-driving satisfaction.

He made her wait . . . until he could stand it no longer. Then, swiftly, he entered her, merging their bodies in the ancient ritual of love. And as they rose together, swirling in the sweetness, her love grew with their physical bonding. At the peak she cried out her love, not really knowing she'd done it.

He cuddled her in his arms and held her for a long time before they stirred.

Her lips nibbled at his earlobe. "Banning, that was wonderful. You make me feel complete."

"You're wonderfully sexy," he murmured. "I'd have to be an iron man not to respond to you, Riley."

"Well, I don't know about iron man, but you're pretty strong."

"It's from all those push-ups I was doing this week without you."

"Did you miss me? Really?" Her fingers spread through his hair and rubbed the back of his neck.

"Like crazy." He kissed the curved trail of her collarbone. "I went for a long walk after you left. To sort things out, put them in perspective."

"And did you?"

"Yes. I realize now the people in my life are first, not things like wallpaper and room decorations. People, like Zabrina and you."

In that order, she couldn't help thinking. Zabrina and me. Well, his child was in his life before she was, so what did she expect? "Good. I'm glad you realize that now. Let's go take a shower."

"I'll scrub your back if you'll scrub mine."

"Will you stay the night? Please?"

"Sure. Love to," he said, pulling her to her feet. They grabbed their clothes and ran upstairs to share a hot shower. Later they fixed a bowl of soup in the kitchen and Riley broached a sensitive subject.

"Would you like to see my half of the two-for-one special? My mural?"

"You and your bargains," he chuckled. "Yeah, why not? Where is it?"

"In here." She flipped on the living-room light.

"I guess I was too busy to notice earlier, huh?" he said, grinning.

"I always felt I needed something in here to make the room look larger. Well, what do you think? Is this large enough?"

His eyes assessed the scene appreciatively. "Riley, I must admit, it's beautiful. And no shiny little nails to mar the landscape."

"Please, don't remind me," she said with a sheepish grin. "I timed the sizing on the wall this time. And the glue. But it still wasn't easy. There are a few places that don't match exactly, but you can't tell it because they're all fields of grass."

"You're right about the sense of depth. Makes the room look much larger."

"I'm glad you like it. I realize it's rather simple, but it reminds me of home."

"The farm back in Iowa?"

"Yes, and these two little girls are like Brit and me. We were very close friends growing up. And we used to go off alone, talking and giggling like girls do, picking wildflowers and wondering about the world and what would happen to us when we grew up."

"Do you ever miss that period of your life?"

"Sometimes. Of course I know that not all of it

148

was as wonderful as this picture makes it seem. But the good is what we remember most."

"I guess we're all like that."

"Do you miss not knowing Zabrina when she was this young?"

"Oh God, yes." He looked up sharply, as if the words slipped out of their own accord and he was surprised to hear them aloud. "How did you know?"

"I just felt it. I know you must have tried to see her."

"Yes, I tried. But until she was old enough to question my existence and insisted on knowing me, Kim and her family managed to keep me away." He sat in a chair and hung his hands between wide-spread knees.

"Even after you moved here and became . . . ?"

"Respectable?" He chuckled bitterly. "Yeah. They thought I was still an irresponsible bum, even though I wasn't living on the beach anymore. They couldn't imagine how I'd changed."

"But you have."

"It was a determined effort, Riley. When I was denied access to my daughter I was furious. Eventually I calmed down and did a lot of thinking. I saw myself through Kim's eyes. A devil-may-care, rash kid who took nothing seriously and behaved with reckless abandon. I'd never held a job longer than three months. Now how could a man like that be expected to be a responsible father for a child? So I set out to change all that. Got an education, settled down in a real house, got a respectable job."

She slipped her arm around his shoulder. "And

now Zabrina's coming to see you. I guess the big change paid off."

"Yes, I think so. I can't wait until Sunday. Actually I can hardly believe the day is almost here."

"I'm proud of you, Banning. You're an amazing man."

"Tell me I'm reliable and responsible."

She faced him and put both arms around his neck. "You're the most reliable and responsible person I've ever known." Riley kissed him with great, intense fervor, for she saw his internal pain and loved him more than she'd ever loved any man. Including the man she'd married.

The next day Riley and Banning went back to his house to help finish up last-minute details before Zabrina's arrival.

Riley went from room to room, reeling off the essential items. In the kitchen, she opened the freezer. "Let's see. Plenty of frozen pizza, hamburger patties, hot dogs, and ice cream."

Banning followed her. "And milk in the refrigerator."

"Very good." Riley strode into the living room. "Okay, VCR ready to go and a couple of"—she carefully avoided the word *teen*—"couple of kid movies."

"Do you think they're too old for her? What about Disney?"

"No. They're fine," Riley said firmly, and continued upstairs to the pink, fluffy room. "Now, did you get rid of that old record player?"

"Yes. She's all set up with a boom box that plays cassettes, just like you said."

"She'll love it, Banning."

He looked up at the ill-fated mural. "I still think I should pay you for that . . ." He gestured at the wall.

"Absolutely not. It'll be my gift to Zabrina. Anyway, after what I did to the wall, I'd feel guilty taking your money."

"But you can't afford it."

"It's okay," she said, smiling. "I just added it to the old charge account."

"Riley, you can't keep doing that. Someday you'll have to pay the piper."

"Yeah." She paused for a remorseful little laugh. "In September. Everything comes due then. The furniture, Jordan, and I'm sure the credit-card bill will still be around."

"Riley?" Banning turned her firmly toward him. "What did you say?"

"Oh, I don't worry about my bills, you know that, Banning."

"About Jordan? What did you say about Jordan?"

She shrugged and tried to get free. But Banning held her.

"Riley, tell me."

She took a deep breath and tried to sound nonchalant. "I told Jordan I'd pay him back by September or . . ."

"Or what?"

"Or I'd go into business with him and run that stupid import office for him."

"My God, Riley! How could you agree to anything so rash? You know you won't have enough money to repay him by September. That's thousands of dollars!"

"I will too! I'm determined to hit it big, Banning. And I have a deal pending, one with an industrial park that involves several businesses. I'm going to pay him off, I swear."

"But you've set an impossible date for yourself."

"I don't think so. Why, I more than doubled my volume this week, Banning. Aren't you proud I sold Shoe Mountain?"

"Yes. Yes, I'm proud of that. But you're still so far from your goals. Too far, I'm afraid."

"Don't worry about my financial situation. You just concentrate on making Zabrina's visit the best it can be."

Apparently he did. When he went to the airport on Sunday to pick Zabrina up, Banning didn't invite Riley. She sat at home alone.

CHAPTER NINE

On Monday morning Riley arrived at the office before Banning. She didn't recall it ever happening before in the weeks she'd worked there, but then this was no ordinary morning, either.

Undoubtedly he was having a leisurely breakfast with his daughter, Riley thought, remembering the meals she'd shared in the very same kitchen. Damn it, she'd promised herself not to be jealous. If only Banning had called last night, perhaps even after Zabrina had gone to bed. But he hadn't.

"Well, Spidey," she said with a sigh. "Might as well get on with it." Armed with a fresh cup of tea, she consulted her list of tasks for the week. First on her agenda was finding a place to have her gold-plated shoehorn repaired. The walnut handle had cracked somehow during the wild day when she'd sold all the sport shoes.

She was talking on the telephone to a specialty repair shop when Banning and Zabrina walked in. Had he mentioned bringing her to the office today? Riley couldn't remember his discussing any plans, let alone this one, and she was caught totally off guard.

She used the moments of finishing the telephone call to collect herself before slowly swiveling her chair toward his desk. "Good morning."

Banning looked up from the papers he was sorting and Zabrina turned from her examination of his CPA certificate.

His expression was neutral. No special smile. No movement in her direction. "Good morning, Riley. I'd like you to meet my daughter, Zabrina. Zabrina, this is my office partner, Ms. Dugan."

Riley felt as if she'd been slapped. Banning's antiseptic introduction dashed any remaining hope that she'd be a part of his daughter's visit. For reasons of his own, he did not intend to reveal the personal nature of his relationship with Riley to this leggy adolescent in a denim miniskirt.

"Glad to meet you, Ms. Dugan."

"I'm glad to meet you too." Riley wanted to hate this child who was standing, almost literally, between her and the man she loved. But the girl's timid smile reached out to her, making negative emotions impossible. After all, none of this was Zabrina's fault. "And please call me Riley," she added. Banning might introduce her as Ms. Dugan, but she didn't have to leave it that way.

"Okay." Zabrina tucked her long brown hair behind her ears. "That's a jammin' telephone."

"Why, thank you." Riley noticed Zabrina's fingernails were well chewed. The poor kid had probably bitten them to the quick during the plane ride here. "I like your earrings."

"Oh." Zabrina ducked her head and peeked back at Riley with another hesitant smile. "Thanks."

She fingered the iridescent shell that dangled below her earlobe. "My boyfr—a friend gave them to me."

You've got your father's ears, Riley thought with a pang of recognition. And his straight, aristocratic nose. But those hazel eyes must be Kim's contribution.

Riley didn't dare say any of those things, so she settled for a traditionally polite question. "How do you like Seattle so far?"

"She hasn't seen much of it," Banning answered for her.

Riley imagined she saw a flicker of irritation on Zabrina's young face.

"The plane was late yesterday," Banning continued, "and Zabrina . . . we slept in."

"Yeah," Zabrina agreed, sneaking a look at her father. "I'm usually not up this early in the summer. My hair's a mess because I didn't get a chance to blow-dry it right. But . . . Dad"—she hesitated over the unfamiliar form of address—"Dad wanted us to leave because he has lots of things scheduled for us today, so . . ." She shrugged.

Banning stacked the papers on his desk and stood up. "And we'd better get started. Your hair looks just fine for taking a ferry ride. It'll get blown all over the place, anyway."

"It's not fine. The back's a wreck. My curling iron didn't heat up enough. Look at this." She grabbed a fistful of hair and held it out for Riley's inspection. "See how straggly?"

Riley remembered the woes of hairstyles gone awry. Oh, how she remembered. "Well, I don't—"

"I have the solution," Banning said briskly, opening a drawer and taking out a rubber band. "Here. If it's bothering you so much, put it in a ponytail."

Zabrina recoiled in horror. "A ponytail? Gross!"

Banning dropped the rubber band back in the drawer with a sigh of frustration. "Just a suggestion."

Riley didn't know who to feel sorrier for— Zabrina, Banning, or herself. As she'd feared, Banning had a full-blown teenager on his hands, complete with a boyfriend back home.

No amount of wishing on Banning's part would transform Zabrina back into a little girl. Even fathers who'd lived with their daughters since the girls were born found these years "considerably taxing," as Riley's father used to say. For someone starting out fresh, like Banning, communication and understanding could be overwhelmingly difficult.

Riley thought she might be able to help, but no one had asked her, had they? The knowledge hurt. She should be glad if Banning and Zabrina had a miserable time together. But Riley knew she wouldn't be glad at all.

"I guess we'll take off," Banning said, scanning his desk one more time. "I'll be back this afternoon to check my messages. If anyone comes in . . ."

"I'll tell them you're taking some vacation time with your daughter," Riley said smoothly. She wouldn't allow Banning to see how he'd wounded her by pretending to Zabrina that Riley was only a business associate.

156

Zabrina approached Riley's desk and pointed to her shoehorn. "Is that yours?"

"Yes. And it's broken."

"Dad said you sold shoes. Is it made of gold?"

"Gold-plated."

"Pretty fancy." She paused for Riley's reaction. "Get it? Fancy for Fancy Footwork."

Riley groaned and laughed. "I get it. I can see I'll have to be on my toes around you."

"Yep." Zabrina glanced at the Garfield phone. "How do you make calls on that?"

"Go ahead and make one," Riley offered. "You pick up his tail to dial. I'm sure your father can spare a little more time."

Zabrina picked up the receiver. "His eyes open! Look, Dad! Isn't that cute?"

"Uh-huh."

Zabrina replaced the receiver. "I just remembered. I don't know anyone to call in Seattle."

"Then call this number." Riley flipped her card file around to the one she wanted and placed it in front of Zabrina.

"Dial-a-Joke? Great! Garfield's my favorite cartoon," Zabrina confided to Riley.

"Mine too," Riley said. While Zabrina punched in the number Riley glanced at Banning. He reminded her of a magazine model for business suits —handsome, well-dressed, and wooden. Was this the same man who had strummed his ukulele underneath her balcony Friday night? *Loosen up!* she wanted to shout.

Zabrina giggled and hung up the telephone.

Riley smiled. "Good joke?"

"Bad joke. The kids at school will love it. They'll be impressed that I heard it on the mainland. Everyone was jealous of this trip."

Riley decided the girl was deliberately making conversation, as if trying to stall off her departure with Banning. "And I imagine the Seattle kids would be jealous of you, living in Hawaii," she commented. "The grass is always greener, huh?"

"Hawaii's nice," the girl said, hastening to defend her home. "But after all, you've got Hollywood over here, and Beverly Hills, and all those recording studios."

"And Disneyland," Banning prompted.

"Yeah," Zabrina said without much enthusiasm. "But all the kids talk about is Hollywood. Boy, what I'd give to run into Bruce Springsteen or Michael J. Fox on the street!"

"That would be exciting," Riley agreed.

"Breathtaking," Banning said.

Zabrina spread her arms wide. "It would be outrageous!"

"That too," Banning said. "And it's time for us to catch the ferry. I'll be in later, Riley."

"Fine. Have a good time."

Zabrina didn't move. "You two have a really nice office. I like all the plants. What's that funny-looking one with the moss growing out of the wood?"

"That's Methuselah," Riley answered, not caring that Banning was fidgeting impatiently. Didn't he want Zabrina to talk to her? Well, tough!

"The old guy in the Bible with the long beard?"

"That's the one."

158

"I never thought of naming plants. What a great idea! Did you name any others in here?"

"The plant with the hanging stalks is Spidey."

"Like in *Spiderman!* I love it. Any more?"

Riley shook her head and smiled. "The rest are new and I haven't found names for them yet. Maybe you'd like to help me?"

"Sure. I'm good at naming stuff. I'll think about it."

"Great."

"Zabrina, we do have to leave," Banning said, reaching for the doorknob.

Zabrina sighed. "Okay. 'Bye, Riley. I'll let you know if I think of any names for your plants."

"You do that."

Then the door closed and Riley was alone again. Her fingers clutched the cracked shoehorn, and with a muttered curse she hurled it across the room in the direction of the door.

"Banning Scott, you are an imbecile!" she cried. "And I hope that bouncy young girl gives you fits." She blinked rapidly, determined to stay angry and not let any tears slip by and ruin her makeup. Banning wasn't worth it.

"It's you and me, Garfield," she said, picking up the receiver. "And who gives a damn about that man, anyway? We've got work to do."

Quickly she opened a file and pulled out her carefully researched list of the major manufacturing plants in Seattle. The sport-shoe episode had given her an idea that just might help her meet the deadline with Jordan. Despite what was happening in her personal life with Banning, she intended

159

to make that deadline and rid herself once and for all of Jordan's manipulations.

Riley threw herself into her task with a vengeance. Soon she had arranged three appointments for the following Friday, each one with the head of a manufacturing plant. The executives had agreed to listen to her plan to provide safe, comfortable work shoes for their employees at a group discount.

She spent the afternoon scouring catalogs for the types of shoes she would offer during her presentation. If her profit margin was what she hoped, she would have no trouble paying Jordan. But first she had to make the deals.

Riley longed to discuss her project with someone. Hell, not just someone. In the last few weeks Banning had become her friend and confidant as well as her lover. But he was otherwise occupied today and by his own choice had excluded her.

Gathering up her catalogs, Riley took her purse from the desk drawer and left the office, locking the door behind her. In her present mood she decided she'd rather not be there when Banning returned for his messages.

In the next three days Riley had no trouble avoiding Banning. Their paths seldom crossed and their only communications were brief, businesslike notes placed on each other's desks. Riley got the message loud and clear.

To preserve her sanity she concentrated on the presentations she would give Friday. She didn't think beyond her trio of appointments because the weekend promised to be miserably lonely.

Banning and Zabrina were leaving Saturday morning for Disneyland. By the time they returned the following week, Zabrina's visit would be nearly over, but the rift it had caused between Banning and Riley might never heal.

On Friday Riley arrived at the office early to make sure she had all her materials in perfect order for her first appointment. She also planned to spend a few minutes straightening the displays in the van, in case any of the executives wanted a tour. Maybe they'd even buy shoes for themselves today.

The morning was cool, with gray clouds shielding the sun's rays and a breeze blowing from the Sound. Riley left the back doors of the van open to better enjoy the fresh air, and turned the stereo on to bolster her spirits. This morning she had to be up, despite the drain of the last few days on her emotional resources.

She didn't realize Banning was there until she turned to pick up a box of shoes and saw him leaning against the van door, watching her. Her heart did its usual somersault at the sight of him, but she struggled to present a calm exterior.

"Hello, Banning."

"Appointment this morning?"

"One this morning with Maxey Industries and two more this afternoon with companies just as big. The van has to be in top shape today."

"The industry appointments you were trying for?"

"Yep." She glanced at his casual dress. "I take it you don't have any clients this morning?"

"No."

Riley picked up a soft cloth and began polishing the smudges from the glass behind the shelves. "Did you forget some files?"

"No."

She stopped polishing and took a closer look at him. "Banning, you haven't even shaved this morning."

He rubbed his chin absently. "I must have forgotten."

"Forgotten?" She dropped the cloth and walked to the back of the van to stare down at him in sudden concern. "Banning, is something wrong?"

"It's—oh, hell, you don't have time to worry about it. You have an important appointment."

"I have a little time." Berating herself for being such a pushover, she held out her hand. "Come on up."

He grasped her hand, the first physical contact they'd had since Zabrina arrived, and they both felt the jolt of touching again. In the next instant he was holding her, pressing her to him as if trying to make up for all the deprivation they'd suffered.

"Oh, Riley," he moaned. "I've made such a mess of everything."

Although her body reacted to his immediately, her tone was cautious. "Have you?" Riley didn't know if he meant with her or Zabrina. That he still needed Riley was obvious, but if he hadn't explained their relationship to Zabrina, how much did he really care?

"Zabrina says she wants to go home."

Zabrina. After the first wave of disappointment

passed, Riley considered his statement. Would the girl be so blunt? Yes, she probably would at her age. Despite all Riley's vows not to involve herself, her heart ached for Banning. "Why?"

He relinquished his hold on her and stuffed his hands in his pockets. "She doesn't like it here." He paced to the front of the van and dropped into a chair. "She doesn't want to take a motor-home trip to Disneyland."

"Maybe somewhere else, like Hollywood . . ."

"I doubt it." He took a deep breath and seemed to have difficulty with the next sentence. "If the truth be known, I think she . . . doesn't much care for me."

"Oh, Banning, I can't believe that." Riley sat beside him and took his hand. She wished she had the power to wipe the misery from his voice and replace it with the enthusiasm he'd once had for his daughter's visit.

"We don't get along, Riley. You were right. I don't know much about teenaged girls, and that's how she thinks of herself. She mentioned not wanting to be 'cooped up' in the motor home for six days. I think she doesn't want to be cooped up with me."

Riley couldn't bear the pain in his blue eyes. "Let me talk to her."

"I don't think you can do anything. I'm supposed to be picking up her ticket for this afternoon's flight out, but I decided to . . . come by the office first, just in case you might be here."

"Don't get the ticket." She squeezed his hand

and stood up. "Lock up the van and wait in the office. I'll be back in a jiffy."

"Don't expect miracles, Riley."

She gave him an encouraging smile. "Why not?"

Misty rain began to fall as Riley crossed the Evergreen Point Bridge on Cyclops. But she didn't care. What was a little rain spattering her dress compared to the pain Banning and Zabrina were suffering?

And then she remembered her appointments. Even if her talk with Zabrina took only five minutes, and that was doubtful, Riley would miss the first meeting. And she hadn't even called to cancel.

"Damn it, Riley Dugan, you are a fool," she muttered to herself. If she had any sense of self-preservation, she'd turn the cycle around and keep her appointments. So what if Banning and Zabrina didn't hit it off? The girl would go home, and Riley would have Banning all to herself again. Wasn't that what she'd wanted a week ago?

Yet here she was, riding to the rescue, sacrificing her own business future for a man who'd been ignoring her for the past five days. And why was she doing this noble deed? Because she loved the jerk! Cursing herself for being a complete idiot, Riley stepped on the gas pedal and steered Cyclops toward Bellevue.

As she waited for Zabrina to answer the doorbell, Riley again doubted the wisdom of coming here. What could she say to this troubled girl that would make any difference? But she had to try.

Zabrina kept the chain across the front door until she recognized Riley. Then she opened the door wider and smiled tentatively. "Hi."

"Hello, Zabrina."

Zabrina glanced past Riley at the black cycle in the driveway. "You rode here on that?"

"Yes, I did."

"That's terrific. I wish Dad . . . uh, I mean, would you like to come in or something?"

"If you're not too busy."

"Well, I am kind of busy packing."

"That's okay. I wanted to talk to you about something, but I can do it while you work."

Zabrina looked wary and began chewing on her fingernail. "Something about Dad, right?"

"Right."

The girl hesitated before finally stepping back to allow Riley to enter. "Did he ask you to come?"

"No."

"Oh. Well, my room's upstairs, if you want to go up there with me."

"Lead the way." Riley had decided not to say anything about her relationship with Banning, other than to indicate they were friends. Therefore, she couldn't let Zabrina know that the layout of the house was very familiar—heartbreakingly familiar, as a matter of fact.

"This is it." Zabrina ushered Riley into the pink and white bedroom and pushed her hair behind her ears. "But I want to tell you first off that I had nothing to do with how this room looks."

"Oh?"

"I haven't had the heart to tell Dad, but I hate all this pink frilly stuff. I outgrew that sort of thing years ago. The only decent part of this room is the mural."

Riley flushed with triumph. "It looks a little like Hawaii," she said casually as she sat on the edge of the bed next to Zabrina's open suitcase.

"Sure does. That picture gave me hope that Dad and I could . . . well, anyway." Zabrina pulled open a dresser drawer and took several T-shirts out of it.

"Zabrina, your father's crushed that you want to leave."

She became completely still, the T-shirts clutched in both hands. "He is?" she said softly. "He didn't act that way when I told him."

"Would you expect him to? He does have some pride, after all."

Zabrina sank to the bed on the other side of the suitcase, but she made no move to put the shirts into it. "I figured he wouldn't care. He's so—so stiff all the time, I decided he didn't have any feelings."

"Stiff?"

"Yeah. He tries to have fun, but just when I think he's going to let go and do something crazy, he stiffens up again." She shook her head. "And that's not the dad I expected."

"What did you expect, Zabrina?"

She shrugged. "I don't know. Somebody a lot different from him, though." She paused and gazed into space. "I thought he'd be more like his picture, I guess."

"What picture?"

"I'll show you." She got up to dig her wallet out

of a purse lying on the top of the dresser. "The picture's pretty old, but it's the only one I have. I found it one day in some of Mom's things, and she said I could keep it."

Riley stared down at the plastic picture compartment that held a faded color shot identical to the one she'd found in Banning's cookbook.

"That's my dad," Zabrina said, pointing to the bare-chested young man, "and that's my mom. Before I came along."

Riley swallowed a lump in her throat. "They made a nice couple." She wondered if they still would. Banning had become respectable. Perhaps now Kim and her family would reconsider their earlier decision, and Zabrina would have a mother and father, with everything legal and proper.

"Yeah." Zabrina looked at the picture wistfully. "Mom hasn't changed much, except her hair's a little shorter. But Dad's totally different."

"I'm not so sure, Zabrina."

"Oh, yes, he is. Always wearing suits, and behaving like the perfect businessman. Bor-ring. Do you know I brought him a gorgeous Hawaiian shirt and he hasn't worn it once?"

"That's a shame."

"I'm thinking of taking it home again. Unless you'd like a purple and red shirt? It would go great with your dark hair."

"That's a sweet thought, Zabrina, but I'm sure your dad wants his shirt."

"He doesn't act like it. Whenever I bring up anything about Hawaii he changes the subject really fast. Like he hates the place."

Riley thought frantically. "I don't think he does. He, um, still plays the ukulele."

"Dad?"

"Yep." Riley wondered if she'd have to explain how she knew about the ukulele, but fortunately Zabrina didn't ask.

"I can't believe it. But I bet he'd never ride on a motorcycle, like you do."

"Yes, he would." How well Riley remembered those rides together.

"I doubt it," Zabrina said with conviction. "He used to have a motorcycle. The one in the picture. I thought he might still have one. I told . . . I told all the kids my dad was really cool. But he's not!"

"Zabrina, I'd like to see you give him another chance. Don't leave yet."

"If I don't leave today, he'll take me in that stupid motor home. That thing doesn't even have a television. I would go nuts without my MTV."

"I think I can convince him to cancel the motor-home trip."

"But then what will we do for another whole week? I can't take much more of this." Zabrina looked at Riley assessingly before biting on another nail. "I wish you'd go with us when we do stuff. At least I can talk to you, and I can tell you're not boring like Dad."

"I don't know how your father would feel about having me along." Riley was afraid she knew exactly how he'd feel. He wouldn't want the three of them to be together.

"I think he kind of likes you," Zabrina insisted. "He must think *something* nice about you if he told

168

you about me leaving. He wouldn't have told just anybody. I mean, you said he was so proud and everything."

Riley shoved aside her own feelings. "Yes, he is. But he also loves you very much."

Zabrina met the declaration with silence.

"Please stay a little longer, Zabrina. Let me talk to your father. I think the two of you can become friends."

"I don't know."

Riley sensed a weakening of Zabrina's resolve. "But you will stay for a while to find out?"

"I guess. Oh, I thought of a name for one of your plants."

"You did? What?"

"Footloose. That's kind of silly for a plant, which doesn't move around, but I liked it because of your job. You know, selling shoes and everything. And I loved the movie with that name. Did you see it?"

"Yes, and I loved it too. You've come up with a terrific name, and I have just the plant for it. Thanks, Zabrina."

"You know, that's what I thought Dad would be. Footloose."

"Maybe he can be, at least once in a while."

"I don't know," Zabrina said again. "But I'll give it another shot if you say so."

"Good." Riley stood up. "Then I suppose you have some unpacking to do."

Zabrina shrugged. "Oh, well. Nothing's on TV for another hour. I might as well do something to occupy my time."

"I think your dad will be home soon."

"Tell him to bring his ukulele."

Riley looked into Zabrina's hazel eyes and saw a tiny spark of laughter. What a shame that father and daughter had already wasted so many days and hadn't learned how to enjoy each other.

"Can you play, Zabrina?"

"No, but I'd sure like to learn."

"Okay," Riley said with a grin. "I'll let him know."

CHAPTER TEN

Banning waited nervously in the office. He couldn't believe he'd botched everything with Zabrina when it meant so much to him. And now it all hinged on Riley. What could she do? She didn't even know Zabrina. But then, neither did he.

Pacing, hands stuffed helplessly into his pockets, he stopped when a branch from Riley's spider plant brushed his head. Spidey, she called it. She even talked to the thing on occasion, like when she was trying to work things out. *Like now.*

Crazily he wondered if it worked. Certainly the plant seemed to thrive on the relationship. It had sprouted several new shoots—Riley's term was "new babies"—in the weeks since she'd clipped it back to a few bare leaves.

The staghorn fern, old Methuselah, had also thrived, although it was slower to change and grow. Like himself. It suddenly occurred to Banning that he was like that damned fern, thriving on his surroundings, but slow to change. And Riley was like Spidey, growing, changing, sending shoots out everywhere to affect those around her.

Even now Riley was reaching out to his darling Zabrina on his behalf. She'd dropped whatever she was doing to try and fix what he considered a hopeless mess. He snapped his fingers as he realized that Riley would miss her important meeting this morning and she hadn't even taken time to call and cancel. His problem with Zabrina had become her chief concern and she'd dashed off with no more thought to her own business. He knew she needed to make that appointment, desperately needed the new sales.

The least he could do was try to salvage the meeting without having it be a complete no-show, which would not look good for her at all. He strode over to her desk and searched for her appointment book. Finally his gaze fell on the Garfield phone where a sticky note was attached to the receiver. He grabbed the note—"Maxey Industries, 10 A.M." That was it! Quickly he picked up the cat's tail and began to dial.

Garfield's eyes slid open and he seemed to watch with devilish pleasure as Banning diplomatically canceled and rescheduled Riley's important appointment.

In the next hour Banning watered every plant, paced a crease in the floor, and nervously raked his hand through his hair at least a hundred times.

He was acutely aware that this visit with Zabrina was his last chance for a relationship with her for several years. Not only had he missed her childhood, but he would miss her adolescence if they couldn't work this out.

Their only hope would be another chance when

Zabrina was an adult and mature enough to understand the intricacies of a father-daughter relationship. Maybe by then he, too, would understand it. Unless Riley—he turned as the office door opened.

"Hi." Riley gave him an encouraging little smile and then glanced in dismay at the carpet. Water dripped from the hanging plant to a wet spot forming on the gray plush. "I see you watered Spidey. Thanks."

"Overwatered," he grumbled.

"It's easy to do. You'll get the hang of it in time." She grabbed an old towel from her bottom desk drawer and threw it on the puddle. Amazingly, Banning just stood there and watched her.

"Oh? Like I snapped onto a winning relationship with my daughter?"

Riley walked over and took both his hands in hers. "That, too, takes time to develop."

"Well, it didn't take me long to make a complete mess of it."

"You didn't make a complete mess of anything, Banning. You just have to work at it. But so does she. You two don't even know each other. And both of you had incorrect notions of what to expect."

"You're right there. I expected a little girl to come hopping off that plane. When Zabrina, with her dangling earrings and miniskirt, came up to me and said 'Hi, Dad,' I was astonished."

"I was afraid of that," Riley murmured. She squeezed his hands and noticed they were strangely cold and unresponsive. She'd never known his touch to be cool and her heart ached for him. "Let's sit down and talk."

"Is this bad news?"

"No, not at all. We just have to air some things."

"Okay, I expected a little girl and I got a young lady. What was Zabrina's misconceived notion of me?" Banning heaved himself into his desk chair. "Surely she expected an adult man."

Riley smiled at his perception and moved over to her hot plate. "How about some tea?"

"Are you going to talk to me or what?"

"Or what," she said firmly, dropping tea bags into the cups. In a few minutes she returned with steaming cups of fragrant tea. "On misty days there's nothing better than amaretto tea."

"Are you going to tell me what you and Zabrina talked about?"

"Yes, of course." Riley pulled one of his client's chairs around the desk and took a quick sip of hot tea before she started. "As I said, both of you had different expectations of each other. And both of you were wrong."

"So I was all wrong," he muttered morosely.

"No, you weren't *all* wrong, Banning. Anyway, you couldn't be expected to know what she'd be like. Don't blame yourself."

He eyed her skeptically. "What did she expect?"

"Do you remember the photo I found in the cookbook? The one with you and Kim and the motorcycle and surfboard?"

"Yes."

"Well, apparently there are two prints, because Zabrina has one just like it. And that's what she expected." Riley paused to take a sip. "She thought her daddy was a—"

"A beach bum?" Banning exploded. "I've worked for years to get rid of that image and damned if Kim doesn't perpetuate it by giving our daughter a picture that keeps it alive."

"Did you ever send Zabrina a picture of you in a three-piece suit standing in front of your CPA certificate?"

"No, of course not."

"Thank God you didn't, because I doubt if she would have come to Seattle. But, don't you see, Banning, that's the picture you're giving her now? She expected a dad who was—in her words—cool. What she found was a dad who was stiff and uptight and—"

"Well, hell! I'll admit I've been uptight about meeting my daughter for the first time in her life! So I'm not what she expected. I can't help it. This is the way I am now."

"No it isn't. Not really. Not all the time. She needs to have a little fun. And so do you."

"Fun? I'm sorry, but I'm an adult now, with all the responsibilities of an adult."

"Adults can have fun, too, Banning. You can. We both know that. Let your hair down with her. Loosen up a little. You can be serious here with your business. But for your daughter, be a little crazy."

"Are you nuts? That's what ruined things for me in the beginning. I was too crazy, having too much fun."

"No, Banning, I'm not convinced that's what

ruined things between you and Kim. Maybe it had more to do with love, or lack of it, than with your having too much fun or your lack of ambition."

"How do you know what went on between Kim and me?"

"I don't. I just know that if she really loved you and if you really loved her, you would have worked it out. Love has a way of winning."

"You don't know what you're talking about. I did love Kim, or thought I did. And I do love Zabrina very much. I want us to fix whatever is going wrong here."

"That's exactly what I told Zabrina, Banning. That you love her very much and only want to please her. But you didn't exactly know how. And you know something? She feels the same way about you."

Banning looked at her bleakly. "She said that? She loves me and wants to please me?"

"Very much." Riley nodded and fought to keep the tears that swelled in her eyes right where they were. This was very important for Banning and he didn't need a sentimental fool bawling all over the place. "She's agreed to give it a little more time. But you'll need to show her that you know how to have fun. That's all."

"Fun? Like what? We've been touring everything."

"Um-hum, that's great for out-of-town guests. But for your daughter, put on the Hawaiian shirt she gave you and teach her to play the ukulele."

"What?"

"She said she'd like to learn. You two could make up a song together."

"You didn't tell her about that song I did the other night?" He looked alarmed.

"No, of course not." Riley noticed his quick response when he thought she'd revealed something about the two of them. Her heart felt sad. "I haven't told her anything about us. Mostly I just listened. She liked the notion of plunking on the ukulele. You know how kids are. It would be something she could take back to Hawaii with her, something very special from her daddy. Something to prove how cool he really is."

He rolled his eyes. "I'll bet Kim would love that."

"Who cares what Kim thinks now? It's your relationship with your daughter that you're trying to salvage, not the one with your old lover! Or are you?" Immediately, as soon as those nasty words escaped her lips, Riley's hand flew to her mouth. But it was too late, she'd already said it. She hopped up and turned away. "I'm sorry, Banning. I didn't mean that. It's just that I want to help you so much and I spoke without thinking. I always did have foot-in-mouth disease."

He watched her quietly for a few moments. God, he couldn't figure Riley out. She was as spontaneous as that spider plant with its shoots going in every direction. He never knew what to expect of Riley or how to interpret what she meant. And now, with his teenage daughter to figure out, he was a wreck. Spontaneous Riley and emotional

Zabrina. Keeping them apart was driving him crazy.

"No, Riley," he said gently. "I have no intention of salvaging anything with Kim. You're right. What we had wasn't really love. Zabrina is the one I really care about. What do you suggest I do about her? She doesn't want to go to Disneyland and she doesn't like the motor home and—"

Riley lifted her head. She could cry again, but this time for a different reason. He didn't understand what she was trying to say at all. "I suggest you go talk to her. Be open and honest. Let ideas flow between you. Loosen up, Banning. Disneyland is okay, but Hollywood would thrill her. And impress her friends. As for the motor home, she's a young lady now and needs a little more privacy than it can provide."

He stood up and began to pace again, running his hand through his already tousled hair. "Okay, okay, you're right. We'll go to Hollywood and anywhere she wants to go! I'll get rid of the motor home and—"

"Banning," Riley interrupted. "Please, don't make another plan without Zabrina. Talk to her and see what she wants. Get her input and give her your opinions. Make the decisions between the two of you. Both of you decide. Then you'll both enjoy it."

"You're right. You're absolutely right, Riley. I need to include her in this." He pulled Riley close and gave her a quick, solid kiss. "I'm going home right now and talk to her and see if I can patch up this mess I've made. You're wonderful, Riley. How can I ever thank you? I'll do something. Maybe dinner at the fanciest restaurant we can find. This is great!" He dashed to the storeroom and rescued the old ukulele. "I'll put that Hawaiian shirt on the minute I get home. God, it's been ages since I've worn one of those things."

Riley blinked as she watched his eagerness grow. She understood that he was desperate to develop this relationship with his daughter and how important it was to him. "Good luck."

He opened the door and looked back. "Thanks, Riley, you're the greatest."

"Glad to do it," she mumbled with a weak wave. She could see where she stood in Banning's life. *Zabrina is the one I really care about.*

He sailed through the door, his feet hardly touching the floor.

Riley forced back unbidden tears. She knew he didn't give a damn about anyone but his daughter right now. And that was understandable. After all, Zabrina was his flesh and blood, his child. Yes, she knew all that and the rational part of her brain accepted it. But her heart knew he had just dumped her while Zabrina was around. Then, when his life was less complicated, and lonelier, he'd turn back to her. And her heart ached with unrelieved pain.

A moment later Banning poked his head back in the door.

Riley's heart pounded with excitement and hope.

"Riley, I called Maxey Industries, the number

stuck on the phone. Is that the one you had the meeting with this morning?"

She nodded numbly.

"Well, I knew you had forgotten to cancel and nothing ruins a business deal more than a no-show. So I rescheduled for next Monday at eleven. Okay?"

"F-fine. Thanks." She gripped the desk behind her to keep her balance.

"He sounded quite enthusiastic about your shoe service and said their committee was eagerly awaiting the meeting with Fancy Footwork. He even mentioned that he wanted to get the agreement wrapped up soon so they could get started. How about that? Great, huh?" Banning winked eagerly.

"Yeah. Great." She swallowed hard. "Have a good trip with Zabrina, Banning."

"We will, thanks to you. See you when we get back."

The door closed again and he was gone.

Gone.

Riley had never felt so alone in her life. Nor so sad about being that way. She knew her feelings for Banning were one-sided. He would turn to her only when Zabrina was gone. Riley was something else in Banning's life to hide, and she knew she couldn't live that way. She had to be a part of all of his life or she'd never be happy.

Their love wasn't important enough to him to admit. It was something to be hidden, something to keep in reserve.

Banning had made it perfectly clear where she

stood. Damn it, he thought he could buy her off with a fancy dinner somewhere. Didn't he know how much that hurt her?

She'd better bow out now, before she got hurt worse. Maybe she should consider Jordan's offer. There was no way she'd meet the unreasonable deadlines she'd set for herself. And if she had to move out of Banning's office, she didn't know where she'd go. She certainly couldn't afford to be on her own. And she couldn't bear seeing Banning every day without being a part of his life. Yes, she'd have to move out.

And since she couldn't afford to be on her own, her only alternative was to let Jordan set her up in a branch office that he'd pay for. She looked up with tears in her eyes. Soon they streamed unchecked down her cheeks.

"Spidey, why did I have to fall in love with someone who couldn't return that love? How did I get myself into such a mess? Why did you just hang there and let me?" She shook her fist at the thriving plant.

The silence was broken only by the sounds of Riley's sobs. And water drip-dripping from the plant to the soggy towel.

Saturday morning brought more gray skies that threatened rain. She hadn't heard a word from Banning, not that she expected to. He and Zabrina were probably heading for the coast highway this morning. Riley had fixed things up for Banning and ruined things for herself.

Oh, she would make it to her meeting with

Maxey Industries on Monday, probably make a whopping sale out of it. She should be grateful that Banning had thought to call and reschedule for her. And she was. But she couldn't stay in his office. She had to leave before he and Zabrina got back.

Damn! Why hadn't she left things alone between Banning and Zabrina? The girl would be back in Hawaii by now and her own relationship with Banning could go forward. Just the two of them.

But Riley knew she couldn't have let that happen. Not without trying everything she knew to help. That's what she had done. Helped. Now she could live with a clear conscience. Miserably. Without Banning, but knowing she'd aided his relationship with his daughter.

She moped around the apartment, trimming and watering her houseplants, trying to forget about Banning and not succeeding. Then she decided to move the azalea tree he had given her out on the balcony so it could receive the natural rainwater. As she scooted it out she heard the rev of a heavy-engined motorcycle. Curiosity made her look to see if one of her neighbors had bought one.

Amazement made her grip the balcony railing for support.

The man swinging his long leg over the broad black seat of the shiny black Yamaha was Banning!

Riley could hear her doorbell ringing and ringing before she could pry her hand from the railing. Mentally she tried to pull herself together before swinging the door open. "Banning! Why . . . what . . . whose . . . where's—" She clamped her mouth closed, realizing she was making no sense whatsoever.

"If you'll let me in, I'll answer all those questions and more."

She stepped back just as a crack of thunder warned of the pending storm. Riley wasn't sure if the storm was outside the apartment or inside her own heart. She only knew she didn't want to see Banning again, didn't want to be with him any longer than necessary. Her nerves couldn't stand the strain.

"Zabrina didn't go back, did she?" Riley asked, joining him in the living room.

His gaze swept the mural with its two little girls wandering in the middle of an endless field. "You know, you were right about Zabrina. I lost her childhood and I'll always regret it, but I'm working on the present and so is she."

Riley felt like stamping her foot and screaming. Instead, she cleared her throat and asked, "Will you please tell me what's going on? Why are you here?"

He turned around to face her. His arms hung limply by his sides, his large hands flexed impatiently; his whole body looked tense, ready to spring. Coiled tightly. His jaw twitched nervously.

"Banning, what's wrong? Is Zabrina all right?"

"She's fine. Ann took all the kids to a Phil Collins special showing for a couple of hours. Zabrina was excited about that. So I came by to . . ." He took a tentative step forward. "To tell you what happened when we talked. Aren't you curious?"

"Yes, of course. But I expected you and Zabrina to be chugging down Highway 101 by now."

"No, not without you."

Riley felt herself sway and placed a steadying hand on the back of a chair. "W-what?"

"I said, not without you, Riley. But I'm not presuming anything. I've learned my lesson there. We'll talk it over and I'll see what you want to do about our love. Of course what I'd like is for us to get married as soon as possible, but that's up to you. Now, Zabrina and I would like you to go with us down the coast. It would be an excellent time to get closer to Zabrina, don't you think? I hope you'll like her because she certainly likes you, Riley. A lot. And I'm very happy about that."

Finally, in desperation, Riley raised her hand and her voice. "Hold it! Go back to the beginning, Banning. What are you talking about?"

"Back to what?"

"The part about . . . our love."

"I love you, Riley."

"You do?" She clutched her wildly beating heart.

"Riley Dugan, I love you with all my heart and soul. It took me half the night to realize that my biggest mistake was trying to keep you and Zabrina apart. You are both integral to my life and I want you to be for . . . well, forever. And I wasn't doing any of us any good pretending our love didn't exist. And trying to put Zabrina in one slot of my life and you in another. We all belong together."

"I . . . I don't know what to say." Riley had never felt so crazy. Pounding heart. Swimming head. Lump in her throat. Shaky knees. She didn't know whether to laugh or cry or faint. Or all three.

"Well, you could say you love me too."

"I do. You know I love you, Banning."

Then, the moment was wild. He was sweeping her up in his arms and swinging her around the room and dancing with her in the field that stretched forever.

And she was clinging to his shoulders and laughing and crying at the same time. She was aware only of saying "I love you, I love you" before his lips crushed hers and they swayed and swirled together. Arms encircling, hearts blending, souls entwined. Riley had never been so happy.

Later they made love, pledging with sweet, solemn words and complete physical dedication how much they loved and cared for and wanted each other. And when the wildness, the giddy happiness had calmed, they talked seriously. His hands continued to stroke her face and hair and trembling body. Her hands touched his chest, trying to absorb the pounding of his heart, the heat from his body as he declared his love again and again.

"If you'll agree to go, Zabrina and I want you to ride down to Los Angeles with us."

"I'd love to."

"On the cycles."

"You didn't!"

"I bought that one out front. She and I'll ride double. You should have seen her eyes as we picked it out, Riley!"

"I can imagine."

"She wants to go to Hollywood and to Disneyland. And to Carmel. She asked if I happened to know Clint Eastwood."

Riley smiled knowingly. "She's still part child, but also part woman."

"She's so beautiful! And I want her to know we're going to be married soon."

"Are we, Banning?"

"You bet. Don't you want to?"

Riley threw her head back on the pillow and studied the ceiling. "Actually, Banning, I hadn't thought about it."

"I love you and I want to marry you. After all, we'll have a teenager in our house occasionally and I want her to know that this is the natural consequence of love."

"Oh, Banning, I don't know."

"Why?" He raised up on one elbow and crooked one eyebrow at her.

"Well, you know I'm not exactly free and clear."

"You're divorced, aren't you?"

"Yes. But I'm a woman in debt."

He grabbed her and lay back on the flowered pillow, pulling her over his chest. "That's no excuse, at least not one that I'll accept. I intend to help you make Fancy Footwork a great success. I have a lawyer friend who'll work on extending Jordan's loan until we can get a handle on our joint finances. Anyway, when you become Mrs. Banning Scott, Jordan will want to disassociate with you as soon as possible. I'll see to that."

She gave him a sly smile. "How about Ms. Riley

Dugan-Scott? I swore I'd never lose my identity again."

"Riley Dugan, I can't imagine you ever losing your identity. I don't care what you call yourself as long as you're mine."

"Banning, did I tell you how much I love you?"

"Not in the last two minutes." He sighed. "So tell me."

"I love you more than anything in the world—"

And he hushed her words with his kisses.

"Brit! Are you sitting down?"

"Riley! Why are you calling in the middle of the day? Is anything wrong?"

"Just the opposite. Everything's right, perfect, in fact. Remember when you said I needed a CPA to keep my books straight? Well, I found one. He's terrific with figures."

"You called to tell me you found an accountant?"

"Um-hum. And I'm going to marry him."

"Marry? Oh, Riley! Is that going a bit overboard to get your books balanced?"

"Oh, Brit, he balances my life beautifully. I can't wait for you to meet him."

"And I can't wait to. Who is he? And what's he like?"

"Banning Scott and he's like . . . wonderful!"

"Your office partner? Hmm, bet that took some fancy footwork. Well, congratulations, Riley. You sound very happy."

"I am, Brit. Never been happier in my life. I know it's a long way, but do you think you and

Harrison could come to the wedding next week? I want you to be my matron of honor."

"Oh, Riley, I wouldn't miss it for the world. I think I'm going to cry. Is it okay for your attendant to sniffle during the wedding if I promise to keep it quiet?"

"You can sing, dance, or sniffle—anything you want to do! It's going to be a happy occasion."

"Tell me about him."

"A hunk in a business suit. Tall, gorgeous blue eyes. He plays a mean ukulele, even makes up corny love songs on it. And I love him so. He has a daughter who is almost thirteen."

"Ooo, difficult age."

"She's darling. Lives in Hawaii with her mother, but is going to extend her visit here for the wedding. Then, next month, we're going to take a delayed honeymoon in Hawaii and be there for her birthday."

"Sounds like you've worked things out nicely."

"I hope so. Well, gotta go. Banning will be here soon. We're going to look at a new office that overlooks Puget Sound."

"Then you're going to keep Fancy Footwork?"

"Heavens, yes! We're thinking about franchising."

"What a brilliant idea, Riley. New York Stock Exchange, here you come!"

"It was Banning's idea."

"Riley, he sounds perfect for you."

"He *is* perfect for me, Brit. Absolutely perfect!"

Riley replaced the receiver with a silly smile plastered on her face. It was a smile she couldn't wipe away because it came from a well of happiness that began filling the moment Banning had claimed his love. Each time she saw him she felt as if the love in her heart would overflow and never run dry. She had never been so happy and knew instinctively their love could only grow stronger with the commitment of marriage.

When Banning arrived and swept her into his arms, her love bubbled to the surface and overflowed.

"What's this? An unhappy bride-to-be?" His finger traced the tear that dared to surface. "Isn't Brit going to be able to make it?"

"Oh yes, she and Harrison are coming. And Zabrina. And all of my family from Iowa will be there. So my favorite people in the world will be with us for the most important day of our lives. I'm extremely happy. I love you so much, Banning, I just can't hold it in."

"Zabrina is outside waiting or I'd suggest we stay here and work on this overflow of love," he said, nuzzling her neck with eager kisses.

"We have the rest of our lives to work on the overflow," she murmured, returning his kisses.

He drew her closer, his arms encircling her, his body bracing her, his heart pounding against hers, and she could feel their love for each other reaching the brim and overflowing. Together. Forever. Perfect.